DEATH IN DONEGAL BAY

DEATH IN DONEGAL BAY

by
William Campbell Gault

Walker and Company
New York

First published in the United States of America
in 1984 by the Walker Publishing Company, Inc.

Published simultaneously in Canada by John Wiley & Sons
Canada, Limited, Rexdale, Ontario.

ISBN: 0-8027-5591-7

Library of Congress Catalog Card Number: 83-40429

Printed in the United States of America

10 9 8 7 6 5 4 3 2 1

For Bill Pronzini
good writer, avid collector, stalwart friend

Chapter One

ALAN Arthur Baker had never hit it big in the field he chose for his lifetime career. The field was larceny. He had made his first appearance in court at the innocent age of seventeen. The charge was selling bogus location maps of the homes of movie stars in Hollywood and adjacent areas.

Selling these maps was not in itself unlawful. But Alan's maps were several decades old; he had inherited them from an uncle who had been in the same business as a youth. Most of the stars had moved by the time Alan hit the streets. Quite a few of them had died.

The complainants—a vindictive and elderly couple visiting from Illinois—must have hoped for punitive rather than compensatory damages from Alan. They appeared in small-claims court without an attorney.

The case was dismissed without penalty. Alan had taken the precautionary step of buying a rubber stamp to update his avuncular inheritance. The stamp bore the single word *Historic* in print small enough to fit between *The* and *Fabulous* of the original title. The couple from Illinois might have had sight too dimmed by time to read it. The original title had been "The Fabulous Homes of All the Famous Cinema Stars." Alan had made them historic.

He had gone on from there to other small con scams and had become a minor local celebrity. I had grown up in Long Beach, so I was not aware of his reputation when we first met.

I was in my second season with the Rams and being paid more

than I was worth. Four years at Stanford had not made me as sophisticated as I imagined myself to be.

It was over drinks at Heinie's that Alan explained to me how short the life of the professional athlete was, how bleak the years of retirement were—unless he prepared for them. Two days later, I gave him a check for five thousand dollars to be invested in Stadium Mutual Funds, of which Alan claimed to be the financial adviser.

He was more than the adviser; he was the total organization. When it was forced into bankruptcy, Alan escaped with two years of probation on his promise to a tolerant and gullible judge that he would make complete restitution to the investors.

Considering the history of our relationship, I was surprised when he phoned me in San Valdesto on an unseasonably hot June morning.

"Remember me?" he asked.

"Too well. Where are you calling from?"

"In town. I live here now."

"I'm sorry to hear it. What's your latest con?"

"What a thing to say! Jesus, Brock, you were the very first investor to get his money back!"

"And why was that?"

"What do you mean, why? I promised and I paid."

"You don't remember the scene in your office?"

"Dimly. That was a long time ago. I remember you said something about my back."

"That's right. I told you to come up with five thousand dollars in twenty-four hours or learn to live with a broken back."

"Dear God! Mr. Macho. Big man, now, aren't you? You inherited a wad from your uncle. My uncle left me a trunk full of maps. At least I made it on my own."

"Alan!" I said sternly, and started to laugh.

"That's better," he said. "Look, I'm not working a pitch on you. I want to hire you. I need a detective."

"Sorry. I'm retired."

"Sure you are! You have worked on three cases up here since you claimed you were retired."

"For free," I said. "For emotional reasons. I don't do it for pay anymore."

"That figures. You always were an economic idiot. Well, could you recommend any other agency in town?"

"Wouldn't I be doing them a disservice? How could I be sure they would get their money?"

"They could check my credit or they could get it up front. You're not a forgiving man, are you?"

"I guess not. What kind of work—divorce?"

"No. But...checking on my wife. I think she's in trouble, not messing around. I don't want to divorce her. I love her."

"Would that be the former Joan Allingham?"

"Hell, no! That was my restitution to her old man. He had a quarter of a million in the fund. Where was I going to come up with that kind of money in those days?"

"He settled for you marrying his daughter?"

"He did. You never met Joan, or you would realize he got the better part of the deal. We were divorced two years ago. I tell you, Callahan, I had a lot of miserable years before she would agree to the divorce."

"How much did it cost her?" I asked.

Silence on the line. That had been a low blow.

And then I remembered that Corey Raleigh, the boy detective, had not been doing well lately. I said, "There's a young investigator I know in town who might be interested. He's really sharp. Give me your phone number and I'll have him call you."

"I could go to his office."

Corey's office was in the garage of his parents' home. I didn't want Baker to discover that and chintz Corey out of his honest day's wages. I said, "He's hardly ever in his office. He's been very busy lately. I'll have him phone you."

"Okay." He gave me his phone number and added, "Believe me, Brock, I never meant to cheat you."

"Forget it," I told him. "I got my money back. I've been hurt worse by honest men since my uncle died."

I had. By stockbrokers. I should have used my broken-back approach with them. I phoned Corey and gave him Baker's number.

"Is he rich?" Corey asked.

"I don't know. Why do you ask?"

"So I can charge him accordingly."

"Corey," I warned him, "honest investigators have a standard fee for all of their clients."

"That's their problem," he said. "What part of town does he live in?"

"I don't know, but I'm sure he will tell you. Now, you be careful, damn it! This Baker used to be a con man."

"Okay, okay! Don't get all steamed up. This isn't the weather for it."

The Santana wind from the desert had been blowing for two days, setting new June heat records for both days. The forecast was for more of the same. Corey's nine-year-old Plymouth was not air-conditioned. No matter what he charged, he would be earning his pay, sitting and watching, waiting and sweating.

I put on my trunks and went out into the pool to soak. Where had Baker learned about my inheritance and about the three cases I had worked on since moving to San Valdesto? Had he been keeping a book on me? Was he trying to trap me into some kind of revenge con with his call?

From the edge of the pool, a familiar voice asked, "What are you mumbling about?"

It was Jan, my wife. It was the same Jan, except for her hair. I stared at her. "What are you doing home?"

"You know I wasn't going to work today. It's too hot. Audrey closed the shop. I told you this morning I was going to the hairdresser."

"You didn't tell me you were going to do that."

"You don't like it?"

That lustrous black hair of hers that she had worn so tightly coiffed, with a part in the middle and a bun at the back, was now a hemisphere of tightly curled ringlets, Little Orphan Annie style.

She seemed happy with it; what could I say? "I think I'm going to," I said. "It was the change that threw me. Put on your suit and come soak with me."

She smiled. "Do I need a suit?"

"Unfortunately, you do. Mrs. Casey told me she would be back by eleven o'clock."

Mrs. Casey was our housekeeper, a morally rigid woman. "I'll put on my suit," Jan decided.

Mrs. Casey ate lunch with us in the shade of the overhang next to the pool. I told them about Baker's phone call and my suspicions.

"So that's what you were mumbling about," Jan said. "Are you turning paranoiac?"

"Realistic would be a more accurate word. Don't forget I once threatened the man. And where did he learn my recent history—and why?"

"I don't know. You should have asked *him* that."

Mrs. Casey nodded. "That's right."

"Aagh, you two!" I said, having no better reply.

They stayed in the shade after lunch, playing gin rummy and drinking iced coffee. I stayed in the pool. Mrs. Casey's moral code is not as strict as the Baptists' when it comes to gambling. She is a devoted bingo-playing Roman Catholic.

Corey and Alan—there was a pair that deserved each other. But Corey couldn't bat in Alan's league, not yet. I soaked and thought and began to worry. If Alan needed a private investigator, I was certainly an unlikely first choice—for him.

The weatherman had called it wrong. The Santana died at two-thirty; the cooling breeze from the ocean replaced it. I dressed, and looked up the address of Alan A. Baker in the phone book. He lived in our area, in Montevista, but in a more expensive section of it.

"Where are you going?" Jan asked.

"Over to Baker's house. I want to talk with him."

"The phone is still connected."

I stared at her. "What is this, an inquisition? I thought we had this question of my working my way settled some time ago."

"Don't be angry," she said. "We did. It's only that Alan Baker seems to be too tricky for—" She shook her head. "I mean, I don't think he's worth your time, Brock."

I grinned at her. "That's not it. You think he's too sharp for me. You're afraid he's going to con me again."

"No," she said.

"I want to talk with him face to face," I explained. "I want to watch his shifty eyes. Mostly, I just want to be sure that Corey won't be getting into trouble."

She studied me doubtfully and then looked at Mrs. Casey. Mrs. Casey shrugged. They don't always understand me, those two. They love me, but they don't understand me.

Baker's house was on Reservoir Road, on a hummock overlooking the Pine Valley Country Club. It was a big place, of fieldstone, with a brown tile roof, set well back from the road. The Mustang snickered as we drove up the long green concrete driveway. The Mustang shares my inverse middle-class snobbery.

A maid in basic black with a rounded white collar answered my ring. I gave her my name and told her that Mr. Baker had phoned me that morning.

"One moment, please," she said, and left me standing there in front of the open door.

She didn't come back. Half a minute later, Alan stood there. "What a welcome surprise!" he said genially. "Come in."

He was tall, he was slim. He had the perfect eyes for his former trade, a candid baby blue. As we walked down the hall, he said, "Thank God that Santana has left us. Why do the locals up here insist on calling it a Santa Ana?"

"A lot of them are new to California."

"But not us, huh, Brock? We're natives."

He was setting me up early, establishing a common bond. We turned from the hall into a study paneled in light mahogany at the rear of the house. "You must have sold a lot of maps lately," I said.

"Same old Callahan," he said. "You are one sarcastic bastard, aren't you? Drink?"

"Not unless you have Einlicher."

"I not only have it—I have it on draft. You were the man who introduced it to me, at Heinie's."

Bond number two. He went to a barrel front set into the paneled wall and poured us two beakers from the spigot. He handed me one and asked, "Is this a social visit?"

"Not exactly. Did Corey get in touch with you?"

"He did. And I hired him. Now sit down and tell me what's on your mind."

I sat in a deep leather chair and said, "I am sure you will admit that I have a right to be suspicious about your phone call. We certainly didn't part as friends the last time we met."

"That's true. But everybody isn't as vindictive as you are, Brock."

"Not as openly, perhaps. And then I got to wondering where you had learned about my inheritance and the three cases I worked on up here."

"I learned that at a poker game, from a police officer."

"A local police officer?"

He nodded.

"Does he have a name?" I asked.

"I knew it, but it's slipped my mind. Sort of a Lincolnesque type of guy, with a craggy face. I don't think he was as tall as Abe was. A Jewish guy, I think."

"Bernie Vogel?" I asked.

"That's the name."

I said, "Bernie knows I'm retired. What was it, a gag?"

"No. I asked him, while we were having a snack after the game, if he knew of an honest private investigator in town. He told me that you were the only one he knew of, but that you were retired. He mentioned the three cases you had worked on with him, and he told me about the inheritance from your uncle. He made it clear that you weren't active any longer. But I took the chance and phoned you, despite that." He sipped his beer. "Next question?"

"Did you tell him that you knew me?"

He shook his head. "I didn't want to explain to a police officer why I knew you. You can understand that, can't you?"

I nodded.

He smiled. "Vogel probably figured he owed me something. He got into me for four hundred dollars. He's a whiz at poker, isn't he?"

I nodded again.

He smiled again. "Speechless? You?"

"I can't think of any other questions," I explained. "Well, maybe one. This job you hired Corey for—is it dangerous?"

"It shouldn't be," he said. "My wife seems troubled about something lately. There were two times she lied about where she had been. The chance of there being another man involved is remote, but—"

"That's enough," I said. "It's Corey's case and none of my business." I stood up, getting ready to leave, when a woman appeared in the doorway.

"I don't like to interrupt, Alan," she said, "but our appointment is for four o'clock."

He frowned. "What appointment?"

"With the attorney," she said. "With Mr. Farini."

"Oh, yes. I'd forgotten. Felicia, this is Brock Callahan, an old friend from Los Angeles who lives up here now."

She smiled at me. "We've met before, but you probably don't remember it."

"Guilty," I admitted.

"It was at a party at Jan Bonnet's house in Beverly Glen," she explained, "years ago. Weren't you a baseball player at one time?"

"Football," I said. "I find it hard to believe that I would ever forget you, Mrs. Baker."

She sighed. "You had eyes only for Jan that night. My name was Rowan then. Mike Anthony brought me to the party. You remember him, I'll bet."

"I do. He was ranked number three in the middleweight division at the time. Whatever happened to him?"

She shrugged. "I have no idea. And Jan?"

"She married me," I said.

"Lucky, lucky girl!" she said, and winked at me.

"Enough," Alan said petulantly. "We'll be late for our appointment. It was good seeing you again, Brock. I'm sure you can find your way out."

Chapter Two

Down the long driveway, back to Reservoir Road. How could I forget a svelte redhead with green eyes and high cheekbones? They had flooded the dreams of my adolescence. Was I getting senile?

Alan had seemed confident that there was no other man involved in Felicia's lies. Was he getting senile, too?

They had an appointment with Joe Farini, the most expensive and least reputable criminal attorney in town. Why?

Our brief respite from the heat was over; the wind was coming from the desert again. I considered driving down to the station to have a talk with Vogel or over to Corey's to counsel him. But it was too damned hot. My car, like Corey's, was not air-conditioned.

Jan was back in the pool when I got home. I went to the den, which was air-conditioned, and dialed Corey's number. There was no answer. I dialed his parents' number and Mr. Raleigh answered.

He didn't know where Corey was, he told me, but he had said he would be home for dinner. He asked, "Is he in any kind of trouble?"

"Not that I know of. Why?"

"With him, that's my standard question. I'll have him call you as soon as he gets home."

I phoned the station and Bernie was there. I asked him, "Who appointed you my public-relations man?"

"What the hell are you talking about?"

"Giving Alan Baker my name and history. Do you know what he is?"

"The second worst poker player I've ever met, after you. What else is he?"

I was about to relate my history with Alan but decided that wouldn't be cricket. I said, "He was known as a very slick operator down in Los Angeles."

"So were you. Calm down, you hothead! I told him you were no longer active. I made that clear to him. I had no idea he would try to hire you. By the way, did he hire you?"

"You know better than that."

"And you know more than you're telling me. What's going on, Brock?"

"Only my petty annoyance. It must be the heat. I apologize, Bernie."

"For the second time, what is going on?"

"Nothing, I hope. If I learn more, you'll be the first to know."

"I had better be. Your apology is accepted."

"I'm so glad!" I said, and hung up.

Jan was again in the shade of the overhang when I went out. "Well, Hawkshaw," she asked, "what did you learn?"

"I learned that Baker is married to the former Felicia Rowan. Do you remember her?"

"Only by reputation." She frowned. "Wait—I think Mike Antonio brought her to a party at my house one night."

"He did. She remembers it, and me. Why did you call him Antonio?"

"Because that was his name at Hollywood High. He was president of our senior class. He changed his name to Anthony when he started to box."

"And her reputation?" I asked.

"At the level where she operated, I guess you would have to call her a *demimondaine*. At the less expensive level, a hooker would be the word. How is it that she remembered you?"

I shrugged.

She studied me suspiciously. "Was Mr. Baker home?"

"Of course! How high did Anthony go? He never got a title shot, did he? He never fought the champion of his division?"

"I have no idea," she said. "I didn't follow his career. The last I heard, he was a bartender somewhere." She mopped her forehead with a towel. "Is it too early for a drink?"

"Not if we drink them slowly."

We sat and sipped our vodka and tonics and thought our separate thoughts. Jan was probably wondering if Alan had been home. I was worrying about Corey. He could be in over his head.

He phoned when Jan was taking her shower. "What's on your mind?" he asked me.

"You. I don't like that set-up. I understand Baker hired you."

"That's right. I start tomorrow. What's wrong with the set-up?"

"I'm not sure. I'm...just uneasy about it."

"Brock, I'm a big boy now. How am I ever going to get a downtown office with the penny-ante jobs I've been working? He gave me a five-hundred-dollar retainer!"

"Okay. Keep your wits about you. You are dealing with a slippery man. And if the going gets sticky—"

"I'll call on old Uncle Brock, natch. Where else can I find free help? I'll be careful. I promise."

What was he to me? I was too young to be his father and he already had a father. I guess Arthur Miller said it best: They are all my sons.

Night came on, but the temperature in the house dropped very little. There was no breeze, the air too ominously quiet— what the superstitious natives call earthquake weather. Brush fires all over the southern counties dominated the eleven o'clock news on the tube. Thirty-eight homes had been destroyed in Los Angeles County, twelve in Orange County, none (so far) in San Valdesto County.

Jan and I slept in the den that night, one of the two air-conditioned rooms in the house. The other was Mrs. Casey's room, one of the many fringe benefits of her employment. She knew how to take advantage of my addiction for Irish stew.

Was I worried about Corey, or was it envy I was feeling? Getting grounds for divorce had never been my favorite assignment—only slightly more interesting than credit checks. This case was shaping up to be more interesting than either of those.

A con man who had married an heiress under duress, divorced her and married a high-echelon hooker? Investigating that had to be more fun than splashing around in a backyard pool. And Baker may have been telling the truth; grounds for divorce may not have been his reason for hiring a private detective. Nobody lies *all* the time. Why, then, was he having her followed? That was the intriguing question.

I didn't dwell on the questions over the weekend. I played golf. But maybe in my unconscious mind I was thinking about them. For whatever reason, I shot my worst eighteen-hole rounds of history. Which made Monday the wrong time for Jan to ask, "Golf again today?"

"Not in this heat."

She smiled. "And not after the way you played with me yesterday. You're restless, aren't you?"

"Yup. The weather and the golf combined, I suppose. Do you have to go to work today?"

She nodded. "I have an appointment with a client at ten o'clock. Maybe you should have said yes to Mr. Baker."

"Maybe."

"Why," she asked, "would any man marry a prostitute, especially a man as cunning as he seems to be? Could it be compassion, maybe love?"

"I don't know. Maybe she told him, 'No more until we're married.' It's even possible that he was telling the truth; it might have nothing to do with infidelity."

"That's a lot of maybes, isn't it? You used to relish those kinds of cases."

I studied her suspiciously. "Why this sudden urge to get me back to work? You never approved of my trade before we were married."

"I understand you better now," she said. "And I love you even more. I want you to do anything that will make you happy."

"Don't fret about me, honey. Once this absurd weather goes away, I can get back to golf."

"Golf will never be enough for you," she said. "The real golf addicts play in typhoons and hurricanes. Why don't you catch up on your reading?"

"A very sound idea."

The work ethic, that is the curse of the middle class. If I had inherited ten times the money I had inherited, I still would be a middle-class middlebrow. As Heinie had explained to me during a philosophical interlude in his bar, no matter how much wealth some men accumulate, their shoes still turn up at the toes.

There were a half dozen current best-sellers in the den that I had sampled and found wanting. Some sage should explain to these hacks that sex is not a spectator sport, except to voyeurs. Their sales figures would indicate the voyeur population in this country is enormous.

Back to the legendary heroes of my formative years, back to Hemingway and Steinbeck and Fitzgerald. I was deep in my umpteenth reading of *The Great Gatsby* when the phone rang.

It was Bernie. "I've been checking the background of that Alan Baker and his wife."

"Why?"

"Why not? You were the man who alerted me. Some history they have, right?"

"Nothing that should interest a homicide detective. I don't remember mentioning his wife to you."

"You didn't need to. She's famous—in her way. And I got a report this morning that they went to see Joe Farini yesterday."

"Who would report that to you, and why?"

"We have a reason, at the moment, for keeping him under surveillance."

"What reason?"

"That would be police business. I phoned to find out if you recommended any other agency in town to Baker."

"That would be private investigator business," I said. "Thanks for calling, Bernie, and good-bye."

"Wait, damn you!" he said. "What's with you lately? You got boils or something?"

"I'm allergic to police arrogance," I explained. "I tell you everything. You tell me nothing. I pay your salary, buddy."

"No, you don't," he said in his patient voice. "You live in the county. I work in the city." A moment's silence. "All right! We don't know what Farini is up to, if anything. All we have are rumors, so far, from a possibly unreliable snitch who has reason to hate Farini. If we learn more, and you want to know, I'll tell you about it over some of your expensive Scotch some evening. Now you."

"I recommended Corey Raleigh."

"That punk?"

"He is not a punk. He is a mature and perceptive private investigator who learned his trade under a master."

"You?"

"No. Hercule Poirot. Is there some other master you can think of in this hick town? He learned under me."

"Do you know if Baker hired him?"

"He did. To shadow his wife."

"Are you going to pay the kid's bail if he gets out of line?"

"I'm sure Mr. Baker can scratch up enough money to pay for a bail bond. Is that all? You interrupted me in the middle of a good book."

"I apologize, sir. When will I learn not to annoy the citizens of the upper class?"

"Screw you," I said, and hung up.

Bernie always has to play cop. He is a cop first, a friend sec-

22

ond. But I guess that is the way it has to be if you're a good cop, and Bernie is certainly that.

There was no reason to connect the Bakers' visit to Joe Farini's office with Alan's husbandly suspicions. There was a reason to suspect Alan had not completely retired from his larcenous profession. Joe Farini confined his practice to criminal law. And also to something more dangerous than that, as an intermediary between the law and the lawless.

That could involve some hairy characters. I had the uncomfortable feeling that I had sent a boy out to do a thug's work. Corey was equipped to handle a case of wife watching. He was neither physically nor emotionally equipped to handle violence. I tried to ease my sense of guilt by telling myself that Alan was a con man and con men rarely indulge in violence. I didn't convince myself.

I climbed into my car and headed for Reservoir Road. There was no Plymouth parked in the shelter of the eucalyptus trees on either side of the Baker driveway. I drove down to the station, but Bernie wasn't there.

I went home and finished *Gatsby*, and those four last paragraphs knocked me on my ass as they always had. The twenties, that had been America's golden age — and they had happened twenty years before I was born.

Mrs. Casey and I ate lunch in the cool den, along with a glass of good Irish whiskey for her, bourbon for me. When Jan isn't home, Mrs. Casey and I live it up.

Then I stayed in the den to make another futile attack on William Faulkner. She went to her air-conditioned room to watch her soap operas on the nineteen-inch color television set that Jan and I had bought her for Christmas.

Faulkner had eluded me again; I was back in the pool when Jan came home earlier than she had expected to be.

"Put on your suit," I suggested, "and join me in a game of underwater grappling."

23

"I'll put on my suit," she said, "but we'll save the grappling for tonight."

A breeze from the north began to drift in after dinner. We opened all the windows to cool off the house and sat in deck chairs on the front lawn.

A little before eleven, Jan said, "Let's not watch the news on the tube. All we'll see are liquor-store holdups, car crashes, fires, and milling crowds chanting hate slogans from the troubled Middle East. Let's go to bed and start grappling."

"If you insist," I agreed.

Chapter Three

I was on my second cup of coffee in the morning when Mr. Raleigh phoned. "That crazy Corey," he told me, "didn't come home all night. His mother was worried stiff! Then he phones us early this morning from Donegal Bay. What is he doing up there?"

"I have no idea, Mr. Raleigh. Didn't he tell you?"

"Not him. *Confidential*, he called it. Huh! But I thought as long as you were working with him, you might know."

"Did he tell you I was working with him?"

"Not right out. When does he ever say anything right out? Let's say he led me to believe you were."

"He had a reason to," I explained. "I did tell him I would help him any time he needed help. Evidently, he hasn't needed it." I took a breath and said, "If he was on an all-night stakeout, he probably didn't have a chance to phone you before this morning. I think you underrate your son, Mr. Raleigh. He is more mature for his age than you seem to think."

"When he gets mature enough to pay us some room and board and rent for the garage, I'll be ready to agree with you. Mr. Callahan, as one adult to another, if you learn anything I should know, you'll tell me, won't you?"

"Of course," I lied. "Tell Mrs. Raleigh not to worry."

"I'll do that. She thinks a lot of you. And thanks."

Donegal Bay was a beach hamlet about twenty-five miles north of San Valdesto. It had started as an artist's colony in those long-ago days when land along the coast cost less than a million dollars an acre. The colony was still there, and the area was also a mecca for clam diggers and dune-buggy itinerants. The bluff above the beach held the impressive homes of the latecomers who could afford the current prices.

What, I asked myself, was Mrs. Alan Arthur Baker doing in Donegal Bay? Was she painting a picture, digging for clams, racing a dune buggy? Or perhaps visiting a wealthy lover on the bluff?

This case was getting more interesting by the hour. Jan had called it right; it was my kind of case, full of maybes. The first three maybes were doubtful—but who can be sure?

"Who was that?" Jan asked.

"Mr. Raleigh. Corey stayed out all night and he's worried. I wish he would let Corey grow up. He's twenty-one years old."

"Only chronologically. Do you think something happened to him?"

I shook my head. "He phoned home this morning from Donegal Bay. He must have followed Felicia Baker up there."

"And spent the night with her?"

"Watching her, not wooing her!"

"I know. It was my little joke. Why don't you run up to Donegal Bay and question your protégé?"

A little joke followed by a little rhyme; my bride was chipper this morning. Grappling often had that effect on her. I said, "He's probably on his way home by now—and it's none of my business."

She smiled.

"What's funny?" I asked.

"Your little joke. Let Mrs. Casey know if you're not going to be home for lunch. And now I must trudge off to my day of labor."

She trudged off to her day of labor in her little Mercedes, and I went into the den to resume my remedial reading. I had lasted six rounds with Faulkner yesterday before throwing in the towel; how many rounds could I go against Joyce?

None. I couldn't concentrate. I phoned the Baker house and the maid answered. I identified myself and asked for Alan.

Mr. Baker wasn't at home, she informed me. "He went to Los Angeles early yesterday morning and we are not sure when he will be back. He'll be phoning here this afternoon to tell us. Perhaps you could call back tonight?"

"Could I speak with Mrs. Baker?"

"Mrs. Baker is not home, either. She is visiting friends in Lompoc. Would you like to leave a message?"

"Yes. Please tell him I am worried about a young man we both know. He'll know who I mean. The young man's father is worried about him."

Five minutes later, I decided to do what Jan knew I would. I told Mrs. Casey I wouldn't be home for lunch. I told her that if a man named Baker phoned this afternoon, she should tell him I was out playing golf.

She looked at me suspiciously. "Is that a lie?"

"Yes. But it's only a venial sin, not mortal. It's not even venial enough for three Hail Marys."

"And what if Mrs. Callahan wants to know where you are?"

"She'll know. It was her suggestion."

School was out. It was vacation time, and Highway 101 was loaded with vacationers, heavy with campers and house trailers. The petroleum shortage had turned into a petroleum glut and we were back to Mr. Veblen's conspicuous consumption.

The Donegal Bay off-ramp was wide, the road it led into was narrow and pitted with potholes. I turned under the freeway and started to climb gradually toward the sea. It was a small rise. From its crest, the spread of Donegal Valley lay before me. It was studded with wild mustard blossoms and about a dozen large ranches.

The climb was steeper and longer coming out of the valley. A cool breeze from the ocean drifted into the car about half-way up the grade. There had been avocado trees or cattle on most of these ranches at one time. Several of them were still working ranches; the others had been converted to leisurely spreads for the horsey set.

The road grew wider as I neared the top. At the bluff end, an even wider and unpitted macadam road lined with olive trees intersected it. This was the road that served the large homes looking down on the town and the sea.

I drove along it slowly but spotted no nine-year-old Plymouth. At the far end, the road narrowed and started its steep and sharply curved descent to the town and beach below. I stayed in low gear all the way down.

The main street of the town ran laterally with the beach; the five side streets that crossed it extended for only a block on each side. Back and forth I drove, covering every house. Corey's car was not in sight.

He was probably home by now. I was about to turn for home myself after I had covered the final street. But then I saw the sign that read *Einlicher On Tap*.

It was a weathered building of unfinished barn siding with a shake roof. An immense rust-eroded anchor was set on a concrete base in the small patch of ice plant next to the parking area. The place was named (of course) the Rusty Anchor.

There were only two customers in the place. One was a tall, tanned, long-haired, blond, bearded youth wearing cut-off jeans and a T-shirt. He was sitting at a corner table with a tall, tanned, long-haired, blonde but unbearded girl wearing cut-off jeans and a T-shirt. They glanced up as I came in and then went back to consuming the immense bowls of clam chowder in front of them.

The ceiling was festooned with fishnets, the rough wooden walls were adorned with dried multicolored kelp. The man behind the bar could have passed for Clark Kent, except for the scar tissue over one eye and a slightly cauliflowered ear. That should have been the tipoff, but it had been a long time since I had seen Mike Anthony in action.

It was the blown-up photographs on the back bar that alerted me — Mike standing over Jess Leppert as Jess went down in the third round at Las Vegas, Mike's murderous overhand right slamming Chico Maracho halfway through the ropes in their San Diego brawl.

"Mike Anthony," I said, "as I live and breathe!"

He smiled. "Right. And where have I seen you before? I've seen you somewhere, I know that."

I shrugged. "Maybe at Burke's Gym? I used to spar a little with Charlie Davis there. My name is Greg Hudson. Could I shake your hand?"

He shook my hand and said, "That was too bad about Charlie, huh? He had a lot going for him."

Charlie Davis, heavyweight, had been killed in a plane crash. I said, "That's for sure. He was heading for the top when it happened."

He studied me. "It couldn't have been at Burke's. I didn't train there often. Hey, wait, didn't you used to hang around Heinie's?"

"At times. That could be where you saw me. I never got on a card you were on and never more than four-round prelims. How about a tall glass of Einlicher and one for yourself?"

"Coming up," he said. "It was Heinie who steered me onto Einlicher." He poured us a pair of glasses and asked, "Visiting friends here?"

"Nope. Looking for a place to live. I can't breathe that L.A. air anymore. Do you like it here?"

He shrugged. "I like the air. I could use a little more action. My cousin owned this place, and he sold it to me cheap."

"It might be a little rustic for my wife," I said. "Are you married?"

He shook his head and smiled. "That kind of action I can get even around here. I never saw any need to sign a long-term contract." He reached into his back pocket and pulled out his wallet. He withdrew a business card from it and laid it on the bar. "If you decide to come up here, deal with this guy. He's a buddy of mine. He'll do all right by you."

I took the card. "Thanks. How's your clam chowder?"

"You'll never know until you try it," he said.

I tried it. It wasn't bad. It wasn't good, either. "Good," I said. "How about another couple of beers?"

We had those and then I told him that as long as I was in town, I might as well look at a couple of houses. I didn't add that maybe his buddy would know if Anthony was still messing around with Felicia Baker, the woman who had told her maid (and husband?) that she would be visiting friends in Lompoc.

The blonde and the blond went out with me. They climbed into a dune buggy and headed for the beach. I climbed into my car and headed for the office of Duane Detterwald, real estate, trust deeds, insurance, notary public. Just meeting a man named Duane Detterwald should make the trip worthwhile.

His office was half of a converted beach bungalow. The other half was occupied by a bait, fishing tackle, and boat rental shop.

Duane Detterwald was a jockey-size man with a ferret face. He was clothed in a tan Palm Beach–type suit, a yellow oxford cotton shirt, but no tie. His tan loafers glistened with polish. Or maybe varnish.

"Could you give me a rough estimate of the price range you're considering, Mr. Hudson?" he asked me.

"It would depend," I told him, "on what I could get for my house in Brentwood. I suppose those homes up on the bluff are out of sight?"

"Not any more than the homes in your area. I have only one listing up there. They're asking four hundred and thirty thousand, but I'm sure that they would consider a smaller offer. How large is your home in Brentwood?"

"Twenty-eight hundred square feet. It has three bedrooms, a den, and two and a half baths. It's right next to the Brentwood Country Club. It's paid for, so the buyer can't assume a low-interest loan, but I'd be willing to take back a sizable second trust deed."

He nodded. "I'll phone and see if we can get in this morning."

He phoned and we could. On the small dirt parking lot behind the building, he said, "So long as there's only the two of us, we'll take the little car."

The little car was a Datsun 280-Z, the other a Cadillac De-

Ville. Why, I wondered, would Duane Detterwald have to share office space with a bait store?

Zoom, zoom, the Datsun rumbled, rolling out of the lot. Tuned twin tail pipes... *Duane, baby, what goes on here?*

On the climb up the winding road, I said, "I sure thought Mike was heading for the title."

"So did he. Until he ran into Duke Ellis. Duke was the guy who put Mike out of business. He tore his guts out. I won a bundle on that fight."

"Have you known Mike long?" I asked.

He nodded. "Since high school. I told him he wasn't ready for Ellis. But Mike is one stubborn wop."

"You've known him since high school, but you bet against him?"

"I did. And I told Mike I was going to."

And Mike went into the tank, I thought, *and split the wad with you.* I asked, "How long have you been in the real-estate business up here?"

He smiled. "I had a hunch that question was coming. I came up here three months after I joined Gamblers Anonymous. Don't get nervous, Mr. Hudson. You are riding with an honest broker."

"I'm sure I am," I lied.

The house he parked in front of was more Georgian than Californian, a two-story red brick place with white shutters bordering each window, and fronted by a wide, low porch. Fluted pillars supported the roof of the porch.

"The lady of the house," he told me, "never got over *Gone With the Wind.* But now she's found an even bigger all-frame colonial in San Luis Obispo."

The lady of the house had red hair. Any resemblance to Scarlett O'Hara ended there. She was tall and angular and bony, a woman of about sixty trying to look thirty.

"Duane, darling!" she said. "I missed you at the Ellers' party last night."

"I was out of town," he explained. "This is Greg Hudson, Marilyn. He might be interested in your house.

She smiled at me. "This way, Mr. Hudson."

Cutesy, chintzy rooms, crowded with maple furniture and too many oval rugs and oval-framed pictures. There were four-poster beds in two of the bedrooms. I was glad Jan wasn't here. It was the kind of house she would ache to do over—with an axe.

I told Marilyn, "It's a charming place. But I can't make an offer until my wife sees it. Will you be home this weekend?"

She nodded. "But you'd better hurry. A buy like this doesn't stay on the market long."

Outside, Duane chuckled. "Not very long. I've only had the listing for ten months."

He still seemed amused as we headed down the steep road. About halfway down, he started to chuckle again.

"What's so funny?" I asked him.

"You are, Callahan," he told me. "What's the scam?"

Chapter Four

I said nothing, staring straight ahead.

"Greg Hudson!" he said. "What hat did you pick that name out of?"

"I was thinking of calling myself Duane Detterwald," I explained, "but I was afraid people would laugh."

"Some people have. A few learned to regret it."

"Midgets?"

"You're really nasty, aren't you? I went along with your gag to find out what your pitch was. Hell, man, I must have seen you dozens of times when the Rams were still playing in the Coliseum. Mike was never a football fan. Is he having husband trouble again? You're a peeper now, right?"

"Wrong," I said.

"You were afraid to go up against Mike," he went on, "so you thought you might get some dirt from me. Well, you won't. Mike is my friend."

I said nothing.

"A twenty-eight-hundred-square-foot house in Brentwood and driving a seventeen-year-old Ford? How dumb do you think I am?"

"Dumb enough. That Ford has six thousand dollars' worth of Spelke conversion on it in 1966 dollars. I turned down thirteen thousand for it just last month. How about a guy with a Cad DeVille and a 280-Z sharing an office with a bait store?"

He laughed. "You got a point there. What married woman is Mike messing with now?"

"I don't know. I came to town to look for a friend who is

missing. He was least heard of up here. I didn't find him. I saw the Einlicher sign just before I was about to start for home, so I dropped in. I didn't know Anthony owned the place. He didn't recognize me, and I didn't want to be recognized by the owner of the only bar in town. My friend could still be here, and word gets around in a town this size. That could mean trouble for him."

"Okay, you're beginning to make sense. You *are* still a peeper then?"

"Not on this. As for being afraid to go up against Mike Anthony, you and he can round up all the friends you both have and I'll take you on en masse or one at a time."

He smiled. "I hit a nerve, didn't I? Look, I believe you. And I won't tell Mike who you are. He's got too much mouth. What does your friend look like?"

"Tall and skinny. He's twenty-one years old and he's driving a nine-year-old Plymouth, a gray two-door sedan. His father is worried about him, so I came here. I'll give you my phone number, and if you spot the kid, you can call me — collect. I live in San Valdesto now."

"Fair enough. Now about me. The Datsun is mine, the Cad is leased. I don't need a bigger office. I make a very satisfactory income out of the office I have. I sold two ranches so far this year. You know what the commission was on that?"

"Plenty, with the prices in this area."

"The package went for four and a half million."

"At six percent," I said, "that reads out to two hundred and seventy thousand dollars. You ought to buy that bait store."

"I own the building," he told me stiffly. "My nephew and his live-in girl friend run the tackle shop and boat rental that you keep calling a bait store. They don't pay me *any* rent. Now, God damn you, get off my back!"

I patted his knee. "Okay, Duane. I apologize for the things I said. "I was embarrassed. I...overreacted."

He smiled. "I should have expected that. I've watched you overreact plenty of times on the field. Trust me, you dumb jock!

I'm your fan. Now I'm going to take you over to meet my only nephew. He was a footballer, too. An all-state high-school tight end. He played in the North-South Shrine game."

It was the blond youth I had seen at the Rusty Anchor. His name was Jeff Randolph. He shook my hand and asked, "How are the Rams going to do this year?"

"All right, if they can settle the quarterback question. Are you going to college now?"

He shook his head. "I had a year at S.C. That was enough. This is my life, the surf and the beach and the sailboat."

A girl came out from the storage room at the rear of the shop. It was the blonde I had seen with Jeff. Duane said, "And this, Brock, is Laura Prescott, Jeff's bride-to-be."

She shook my hand and smiled. "Don't mind what Uncle Duane says. We're trying to drag him into the twentieth century."

As we walked toward my car, Duane muttered, "Twentieth century! Don't they think I ever played house? But you can't go on like that forever. What if they have kids? They'll be bastards!"

"They mean a lot to you, don't they?"

"Jeff does. I have no kids. And I like Laura, too." He shook his head. "Oh well, they can change. We can hope."

I gave him my phone number, he promised he would keep a watchful eye open for Corey, and we parted better than we had started. That ferret face of his, that was what had made me suspicious. Why did I trust him now? Maybe he had called it right; I was a dumb jock.

I phoned the Raleighs when I got home and asked Mr. Raleigh if their son had phoned again.

"He did. He phoned about twenty minutes ago from Lompoc and told us not to worry. And the missus and I decided it's maybe time that we stopped being so... so protective. But, as you know, he is an only child and—"

"I know," I said. "I was one, too."

Felicia had gone on to her friends in Lompoc after a stop in

Donegal Bay. If it had been an overnight stop, there was reason to believe Mike Anthony had been her host. Which made the case what it had originally seemed to be—adultery. Which could be grounds for divorce. Yet Baker had claimed that he didn't want one. Why hadn't he assumed the obvious? It's not easy to con a con man. Unless, of course, he's in love.

When Jan came home, I asked her if she remembered Duane Detterwald.

She nodded and smiled. "I remember him well. When he first came to school, the boys called him Weasel. But they soon quit calling him that."

"Don't tell me he scared them out of it, a man his size."

"Mike Anthony put a stop to it. They were inseparable." She frowned. "How do you know how big Duane is? Where did you meet him?"

"In Donegal Bay."

"I knew you would go up there. Did you find Corey?"

"Not up there. But I phoned the Raleighs, and Mr. Raleigh told me Corey is in Lompoc now. Your old classmate Mike Anthony runs a bar in Donegal Bay. I wonder if Felicia spent the night with him."

Jan smiled. "Felicia—does that mean faithful?"

I shook my head. "You're thinking of Fidelia. Felicia means happiness."

"How do you know that?"

"How do I always know? I looked it up."

I was making a lot of assumptions on Corey's case that were based on the obvious. The obvious is one of my strengths (or weaknesses). I was assuming facts not in evidence, as usual. So what? It wasn't my case.

Which Corey made clear to me on the phone just before dinner.

"Some friend you are," he said. "You and your big mouth!"

"Could I have a translation of that?"

"Telling Mr. Baker my father was worried about me, trying to make me look like a punk. When I reported to Mr. Baker from Lompoc this afternoon, he was steamed. I had to talk fast to save my job."

"I didn't tell Mr. Baker that."

"No, you told the maid to tell him. Why the hatchet job?"

"Corey, I was worried about you, and so were your parents. And let me tell you, if you tangle with Mike Anthony, you'll find out I had reason to worry."

"Who is Mike Anthony?"

"The man who owns that bar near the beach in Donegal Bay. Didn't you talk with him?"

"You're not making sense," he said.

"Corey," I asked, "are you still in Lompoc?"

"No. I'm home. Why?"

"Come over after dinner. I have some things to tell you that might help you on your case."

Nothing from him.

"Okay, forget it," I said. "You don't need me. You're a big boy now. Good-bye and good luck."

"I'll be over," he said. "I'm sorry I...blew up, Brock."

"You were entitled," I told him. "I do have a big mouth."

When he came, an hour later, we went into the den. In there, I said, "You first."

This is the way it was: He had followed Felicia's car to one of the big homes on the bluff, a house he later learned belonged to Mr. and Mrs. Duane Detterwald. Because Felicia had carried her luggage into the house, he'd assumed she would be staying for a while. But he couldn't be sure of that. So, instead of driving down to the beach to use a phone there, he had gone back to a filling station on the road that led into 101.

It was the only road into the area and he would be able to watch for her car if she left the Detterwalds. He phoned Baker at a Los Angeles number Baker had given him and reported.

Felicia's car was still in the driveway when he came back, so he took a chance and went down into town for lunch.

"At a bar," I asked him, "with an anchor mounted on a concrete base in front of it?"

He nodded. "You know the place?"

"It belongs to Mike Anthony."

"I'll ask you again—who's he?"

"A fighter. A very rough nut who missed the middleweight crown about two bouts short of a title fight. He is also a former boyfriend of Felicia Baker's."

"Well, he wasn't behind the bar. A woman was tending bar."

At six o'clock, he went on, Felicia and another woman and a man had come out of the Detterwald house and climbed into a Cad DeVille and driven down to one of the ranches in the valley for a big outdoor barbecue. Corey had watched the scene from a higher point in the road.

A little before midnight, the Cadillac had come back up the road and he'd followed it to the Detterwald house. When the lights had gone out in the house, he'd taken his sleeping bag into some shrubbery on the vacant lot across the street and gone to sleep.

When Felicia left the house the next morning, he followed her to Lompoc. He couldn't get the name of the occupants there. He phoned Baker from there, and that's when he got the bawling out. From there, he followed Felicia home.

"What blarney did you feed Baker when he blew up?"

"I told him my grandmother was dying up in Sonora Creek and my father was anxious to get in touch with me so the family could go up there together."

"And he bought it?"

"I guess. I phoned him when I got home and said my grandmother had made a turn for the better, so we weren't going up. I could stay on the case."

"You'll still be shadowing Mrs. Baker?"

"Yes. Mr. Baker is still down in Los Angeles, and he didn't tell me to stop. He sure didn't pay a five-hundred-dollar retainer for two days of work."

"A working day is eight hours," I pointed out. "You worked longer days than that. Are you getting expenses, too?"

"Natch." He smiled at me. "You want it, don't you! You're aching to get knee-deep into this case."

"Not yet," I told him.

It is hard to con a con man. Corey had used the hoariest excuse known, the truant schoolboy's excuse for absence, a grandmother's funeral. I was beginning to understand why Alan Arthur Baker had never graduated to the big con.

Chapter Five

WHEN I had asked Felicia Baker what Mike Anthony was doing now, she had replied, "I have no idea."

She had spent the night with Mike's friend in a town where Mike lived and worked, but she had no idea of what Mike was doing now?

And then the remark of the aging redhead in the Colonial house came back to me: "Duane darling! I missed you at the Ellers' party."

And he had answered, "I was out of town."

If the barbecue that Corey had watched from afar had been the Ellers' party, I now had another scenario. Duane had been out of town. Mrs. Detterwald had phoned Anthony to tell him Felicia was at their house. While Corey was down at the filling station phoning Baker, Mike had put the woman behind the bar and gone up to the Detterwalds'.

The man and two women that Corey had followed to the party had been Mike, Felicia, and Mrs. Detterwald. When they had returned from the party and the lights went out in the house, Corey had gone to sleep in his sleeping bag, Mrs. Detterwald in her husbandless bed.

But Mike and Felicia? Ah, yes...! And then, before Corey was awake in the morning, Mike had left.

It all tied together, but it was still only a scenario, with no facts to substantiate it. Did Duane know what had gone on in the house during his absence? I doubted it; he wouldn't have asked what woman Mike was messing with now if he had.

Which could mean that Mrs. Detterwald was a closer friend of Felicia's than Duane was.

I wondered if Jan knew her. She was in the dining room, sorting out drapery samples on the dining-room table. I went in there and asked her.

She shook her head. "I never saw Duane after I left high school. Girls liked him, but not in any romantic way. He was short and he was ugly and he had acne and he was poor."

"He's not poor anymore," I said, "and he doesn't have acne. Maybe when he got rich, he got lucky, same as I did."

She studied me balefully.

"I am waiting for your indignant protest," I said.

"Don't hold your breath," she told me. "You called it right. You got lucky."

She stayed with her drapery samples, trying to coordinate them with some unholstery samples she had brought home with her. I went to watch Dick Cavett interview William Styron on the tube. Cavett had replaced the eleven o'clock news for us and we weren't suffering any withdrawal symptoms.

There was a strong breeze from the ocean that night, presaging the end of our heat wave. We would be getting back to the standard June weather report that could be taped for most of the month: "Overcast in the morning, followed by clearing in the afternoon, except along the coast."

Jan apologized in a culinary way for her caustic remark of the night before; she made me popovers for breakfast and a Spanish omelet. Mrs. Casey does windows but not breakfasts. They would interfere with her late, later, and still later old-movie shows on the tube.

"Golf today?" Jan asked me.

I shook my head.

"Why not? It's Corey's case now."

I smiled a smile I tried to make enigmatic.

"Don't simper," she said. "You know Corey can't handle it alone."

"If it's grounds for divorce," I explained, "he can have it. I didn't like those even when I needed the money."

"If you really thought it was only grounds for divorce," she went on in a realistic way she has, "you wouldn't have gone up to Donegal Bay yesterday. Brock, follow your instincts! What else do you have?"

"An acerbic wife."

"Acerbic but adoring," she said. "Go, man!"

Go where? She went to work. I poured myself a third cup of coffee and read the *Los Angeles Times* all the way through to the more interesting obituaries. Indolence is the curse of the leisure class.

The San Valdesto phone book had a Donegal Bay section. I leafed through it to *Eller, Christopher, 1481 Ranch Road.*

Ranch Road was the road that led off the highway. Fourteen-eighty-one would be high on the final rise, close to the road that fronted those big homes along the bluff.

And what could I do with this information? Phone the Ellers and ask them if Anthony had been at their party? No. Perhaps I could identify myself in a falsetto voice as the society editor of the *San Valdesto Chronicle* and ask them for a guest list of their recent party? No.

There might be an account of it in yesterday's edition of the *Chronicle.* The paper was still in the living room, but it held no account of the party.

To hell with it. It was Corey's case, not mine.

The financial station on the tube informed me that the Dow Jones Industrials were now down over nine points, the entire market heading lower. Gold had reached a new high for the week, the dollar a new low. It was caused, most analysts agreed, by new trouble in the Middle East.

What had they done with their old troubles—held a garage sale? Those anxious buyers of gold had better invest some of their money in guns, ammunition, and a radiation-proof fort if they hoped to protect their capital from the hungry hordes when the showdown came.

I considered phoning Bernie to ask him what was new on the Farini surveillance and then decided I wasn't in the mood for quibbling. I remembered that Corey's maternal uncle was also a police officer. I had met him once but had forgotten his name.

I phoned the Raleigh house, and Mrs. Raleigh answered. Her brother's name, she told me, was Einar Hovde and he was on the swing watch this week. She gave me his home phone number.

When I identified myself to him, he said, "It's about Corey, I suppose. What trouble is he in now?"

"None, I hope. But just between us, Lieutenant Vogel told me the department has a surveillance on Joe Farini and I wondered if you knew about it?"

"Very little. Corey isn't sticking his big nose into that, is he?"

"Not yet. Bernie is a good friend of mine, but he doesn't always confide in me."

"I can believe it. He's all cop. Too much, sometimes. I don't know why they're watching Farini, but I do know the name of their informant. You didn't get it from me—*remember that!*"

"Of course."

The man's name was Luther Barnum, he told me, and he lived in the Travis Hotel on lower Main Street. He added, "If he decides to tell you anything, don't take it as gospel. He's lied to us before and he hates Farini. Joe sold him out to the DA on a drunk and disorderly charge."

"Thank you," I said. "I'm not involved in any case with Corey, but I do like to keep an eye on him."

"He can sure as hell use it," his uncle said. "Good hunting."

I stopped at a liquor store on the way downtown and bought a pint of blended whiskey. I didn't want to shock Luther's palate with good vintage corn.

The Travis Hotel was almost as old as the city, a four-story stucco building in the meaner section of town. The lobby held two dusty rubber plants in redwood tubs and a row of straight-back chairs in front of the big window facing the street. The odor of the place was a blend of disinfectant, sweet wine, roach powder, and decayed dreams. Two guests were sitting in the chairs, one of them asleep.

The clerk behind the scarred mission oak desk was thin and

old and black. He was wearing a clean white shirt and shiny blue serge trousers.

"Is Luther Barnum in?" I asked him.

He glanced at the numbered board that held the room keys and nodded. "He might be sleeping, though. He sleeps a lot. Room two-twenty-three."

Room 223 was at the end of a long, narrow, uncarpeted hall on the second floor. I knocked.

"It's not locked," a voice from within called. "Is that you, Al?"

I opened the door. A few feet from the open window that looked down on a side street, a small gray-haired man with a mottled complexion and bloodshot eyes sat in a wicker chair. He was wearing a soiled blue flannel bathrobe. His feet were bare.

He stared at me suspiciously. "Who are you and what do you want?"

"My name is Lee Hawkins," I said, "and I'm looking for an ally."

"Make sense, man!"

"I'm talking about Joe Farini," I told him. "That bastard got me eighteen months on a rap that should have got me three."

"You don't look that poor," he said. "Farini never sells out guys who can afford him. What was the rap?"

"Con. Small con. The pigeon drop."

His smile was scornful. "This could be the only town in the state where that will still work. What you got in your hand?"

"Whiskey." I handed it to him.

He looked at the label. "I've drunk worse, I guess. What do you figure to buy with this?"

"Whatever you want to give me. I'll leave, if that's what you want."

"Sit down," he said. "We'll talk."

There was no other chair in the room. I sat on his unmade bed.

"Who told you about me?" he asked.

"A cop I know. I'm not going to mention his name. But if you have something I can use against Joe, it could be worth a few bucks."

"How few?"

"Ten, maybe fifteen."

"Could you go twenty?"

"If it's something I can use."

"How do I know if you can use it? Let's see the twenty."

I took a twenty-dollar bill from my wallet and held it up. I said, "Give me a hint."

"It's about Cyrus Reed Allingham. Have you ever heard of him?"

"Oh, yes." I handed him the twenty. "Go on."

"My cousin is a maid," he said. "She was Joan Allingham's maid when she was married. When Joan divorced her husband, my cousin stayed with her. I think I know why, but that's a different story. Joan lives with her father now, a real mean old bastard. So I get this letter from my cousin. She's really fretting. She thinks old man Allingham is being blackmailed. She knows I hate Farini. So guess who the go-between is."

"Your buddy, Joe Farini."

"Right!"

"Does your cousin know what the blackmail is about?"

He spread both hands, palms up. "If she does, she didn't tell me. What I told you, that's all I know."

"What's your beef with Farini?" I asked him.

"He sold me out, same as you. He ran me up from a night in the drunk tank to three months at Gaspar. That is one crummy cage, Gaspar."

"Why does he do it?"

"*You're* asking why? He throws all his small fish to the DA to build up Brownie points. Joe likes friends on both sides of the law."

"Where does Allingham live?" I asked.

He didn't get a chance to answer. The door opened and a wide young man stood there. He was only about five nine, but almost that wide.

"Who you squeaking to now, Luther?" he asked.

Luther looked at me, back at the man in the doorway, and again at me.

"Who's the punk?" I asked him.

He shrugged. "One of Farini's muscle freaks. I don't know his name."

"You got a name, punk?" I asked him.

"Stand up and say that," he challenged me.

I stood up. "Make your move, punk, and die before your time."

The jerk moved in on me like the Incredible Hulk, arms wide. He wanted to grapple. I grapple only with Jan. I put a right hand into his nose when he got within range. I kicked him in the groin when he backed off. When he bent over to grab for his affected parts, I put my knee into his chin. He went down with a thump.

He lay there, comatose. I said to Luther, "I suppose we had better call the law before the desk clerk does."

He stared at me. "Here? Are you crazy? Nobody ever calls the law down here. Let's throw him out the window and see if he bounces."

Chapter Six

I stayed with Luther until the muscle man woke up and limped out.

"Do you think he'll be back?" I asked.

He shook his head. "I know a couple of cops that are on my side. They'll give him the word."

"There are some cops who aren't on your side, too," I told him. "You have a...doubtful reputation for veracity."

"If you mean I lied once in a while, I did. I can't live on air. That's why I wound up with Farini."

"I'm not following you, Luther."

"Figure it out. Where would I get enough money for him? I always wound up with a public defender. That last time, on a penny-ante drunk and disorderly charge, who walks in to defend me but Mr. Big! And he throws me to the wolves. I found out later that the fuzz set me up. Sort of a revenge, see? I made 'em look bad in court a couple of times with phony tips. They forgot all the good ones I gave 'em."

"I get it."

He frowned. "Wait a minute—how did you know there are some cops who aren't on my side? You a cop?"

"No. Nor a con man, either. I am only an interested spectator. How do you think Farini learned you put the law on him?"

He took a swig from the bottle. "I don't know. Who cares?"

"I do," I said, and gave him another twenty.

I stopped in at the station on the way home, and Bernie was in his office. "Social visit?" he asked. "Or informative?"

"Neither. I've just come from a talk with Luther Barnum. Who framed him?"

"What do you mean, framed him?"

"Sending Farini in to defend him on a drunk charge and poor Luther winds up with three months in Gaspar."

"Oh, that!" He sighed and shook his head. "That was a long time ago. I guess they thought they owed him. Why were you talking with Luther Barnum?"

"That's none of your business. You tell your redneck buddies if they want to play nasty, they should pick on someone their own size. Give 'em my address."

He said quietly, "Sit down and calm down."

I shook my head.

"We're friends, Brock."

"Not today."

"Today," he said, "or never. I mean it."

I sat down.

"First of all," he said, "those men you called rednecks were never *my* buddies, and they are no longer with the department. I was partially responsible for their leaving. Now, second, why were you talking with Luther Barnum?"

"Because I thought there might be some connection with your watching Farini and Baker's visit to his office. I found out there was."

"And who put you onto Luther?"

"I'd rather give you some more interesting information. Sort of a trade? I have to protect my sources, Bernie, just as you do."

"Oh, God," he said wearily. "All right!"

I gave him a full account of my trip to Donegal Bay, added a few of Corey's discoveries, and finished with my kayo of the muscle freak.

He stared at me for seconds after I had finished. "Did you get the man's name?"

I shook my head. "Luther told me he was one of Farini's stooges."

"A young fellow, not very tall, wide as a barn door?"

"That's the man."

"You put *him* down?"

"Ten seconds into the first round. Luther wanted to throw him out the window, but you know me — I don't believe in violence."

"Oi!" he said. "I'll never be able to understand you. If I had your money, I wouldn't even go slumming down on lower Main Street."

"Cut out the poor-man crap, Bernie. I used to believe it — until Elly told me about your real-estate holdings. You *love* to play cop."

Elly is his wife. "She's got a big mouth," he said, "like you. Would you care to give me one of your dumb Irish hunches about what is going on between Baker and Farini and..." He paused.

"And Cyrus Reed Allingham?" I finished for him. "I know about that connection, too. You know, of course, that Baker used to be married to Joan Allingham."

"I do. And he got a couple million in the divorce settlement. But what in hell has that got to do with Donegal Bay and Mike Anthony?"

"There might be no connection. Anthony used to go with Mrs. Baker. Maybe she's still hot for him."

"How do you know that?"

"From Jan. She went to high school with Anthony. On the Allingham end, if Baker got a big settlement from the old man, he must have had something to sell. Otherwise, Allingham's lawyers could have kept him in court until doomsday."

"That makes sense. And now Baker probably wants more. What could he have on Allingham? Hell, Allingham is the kingpin of the moral-majority movement in this state. He's financed a couple of those pukey movies they turn out."

"There has to be a skeleton in his closet. Why don't you ask Luther's cousin if she knows anything."

He looked at me quizzically. "Who is Luther's cousin?"

"An Allingham maid. She used to work for the Bakers. But when they were divorced, she stayed with Joan. Both of them are living with the old man in that fortress he built up in Veronica Village. Luther got his tip from his cousin."

"That bastard!" Bernie said. "He never told *us* that."

"Maybe," I pointed out, "he's lying again. Or maybe he doesn't want a lot of cops bulling in and losing his cousin her job. I guess I shouldn't have told you about it."

"Don't sulk. We're not going to bull in. Cyrus Reed Allingham lives outside our jurisdiction. Are you going to stay on this case?"

"I am not on it," I said evenly. "Corey is working on that end of this tangle. And it comes under the heading of proper work for a private investigator. I mean the domestic part of it concerning Felicia Baker and Mike Anthony. The part that concerns Alan Baker, Joe Farini, and Cyrus Reed Allingham shapes up as proper police work. And you know how many times you have warned me to stay out of that."

"Do I ever!" He smiled. "And how many times have you obeyed me? Keep me informed, won't you, buddy?"

"No way!" I told him. "I'm going back to golf."

He laughed. "Sure, you are. Good hunting, tiger."

All clean cop, that's Bernie. When he has dirty work to do, he farms it out to me. To hell with that! Still...?

Mrs. Casey wasn't home when I got there. I had forgotten to eat lunch. So I sneaked into her kitchen and made myself a cheese, ham, and tomato sandwich. I put everything back exactly where I had found it and took the sandwich and a bottle of beer out to the shade of the overhang.

Were the cases separate or connected? Corey would not have fared as well with Mr. Five-by-five as I had. And getting involved with Joe Farini was no work for a novice. The cases weren't connected, I told myself. At least, not yet.

Cyrus Reed Allingham, Luther had informed me while my assailant was still on the floor, lived in a veritable fortified castle on a hill above Veronica Village, a retirement sanctuary for the overprivileged about forty miles north of here.

I was on the last lap of my twenty-lap pool workout when Jan came home.

"Have you been in there all day?" she asked me.

"Mostly. There's a pitcher of iced coffee in the fridge. Bring it out."

No need to tell her that I had visited lower Main Street. I'd had enough I-knew-you-would at breakfast.

"And your day?" I asked when she brought out the coffee.

"Fair. Mrs. Casey just informed me that you went downtown before lunch."

"What is this, an interrogation?"

"Not at all. She simply happened to mention to me that you didn't tell her you wouldn't be home for lunch."

"You mean she *complained* to you."

She took a deep breath. "Let's not quarrel, Brock. My day has not been that fair. You have a right to remain silent and if you desire an attorney, one — "

"All right, already! I went down to talk with a snitch and then stopped to gas with Bernie on the way home. Damn it, I'm worried about Corey."

"You should be. And I'm glad you are. Why are you being so defensive about it?"

I didn't answer.

"What were my last words to you this morning?"

"Let's see — 'Go, man!'"

She nodded. "I'll repeat them. Go, man!"

I now had her official blessing, and it decided the issue for me. Corey could handle his adultery investigation; I would work on the heavy stuff. If I could only figure out an opening move....

I phoned Corey's house after dinner and he was home. "Busy day?" I asked him.

"Sitting, that's all. She never left the house. What did you want with my uncle? Mom said she gave you his phone number."

"Ask your uncle."

"I did. He told me it was none of my business."

"He was right. I called you to find out about that party you watched in Donegal Valley. Was that at the Eller ranch, up near the bluff?"

"No. About halfway down. The name on the mailbox was Kratzert. Are you taking over this case?"

"Of course not! I happen to know the Ellers, and I thought if you wanted to question them, I could make it easier for you."

"Brock!"

"Corey, believe me, I wouldn't lie to you any more than you would lie to me. The information I wanted from your uncle concerns a different case, I am almost sure. If I learn it doesn't, we'll work together. Okay?"

"Okay."

"Did Mr. Baker come home from Los Angeles?"

"Yup. That's why I have the night off. Maybe we could work together now? You could take the night shift."

"How much are you paying?"

"Same as you paid me last time we worked together—three dollars and sixty-five cents an hour."

"We'll see. Remember now, if things get heavy—"

"I'll call on my muscle," he agreed. "Stay available."

Kratzert...another scenario had been shot down. It probably had been Mr. and Mrs. Detterwald who had gone to the Kratzert party with Felicia. She had not even taken the opportunity to drive the quarter mile or so to the beach to visit her old friend. But maybe Mike had been at the party?

Don't dream up another errant scenario, I told myself. Facts are what make successful cases.

What case? I had no case. Nobody had hired me; I had turned down Baker's offer. I'd had an excuse, even if a lame one, to travel to Donegal Bay. What excuse could I have for going to Veronica Village?

I could call it an adventure, I decided. My mother had taken me to Hearst Castle on a picnic trip when I was thirteen, and I still remembered it. Now that my taste had matured, a visit to the Allingham fortress might be just as memorable when I reached my final adolescence.

Even if I didn't get inside it, it would be a pleasant drive. My disenchantment with Hearst Castle had started when we went inside.

I had Jan's blessing and Bernie's approval. I had the rest of that day and the next morning to compose my opening lines. I would use my own name; Cyrus Allingham had had a season box at the Coliseum when I was a Ram.

Corey and Vogel were right; I had a big mouth. But that was only half of it. I also had a big nose.

Chapter Seven

PASTORAL and peaceful, that is Veronica Village. The homes were medium-large to large. All the lawns were large and studded with flower beds. The shops were small. The board of trustees permitted no supermarkets or chain stores in their village. The residents could afford to pay the full markup retail, and did.

There was nothing pastoral or peaceful about the castle that brooded over the village from a small hill to the north. The outer wall, the living quarters, and the keep were all constructed of immense gray stones. There were two rows of apertures in the circular keep, all of them barred.

The entire area had been part of the Farrow ranch at one time; the village had been named after Cyrus's matriarchal grandmother, Veronica Farrow Allingham. She had been one of the Farrows, a ranch family. The Allinghams had been engineers, specializing in oil-drilling equipment.

The two-lane macadam road that led past the castle was well maintained, threading into the low mountain range in the distance and disappearing into the agricultural valley on the far side.

It wasn't until I came to the end of Allingham's three-hundred-yard driveway that I saw the dry moat bordering the rampart. Old Cyrus was not missing a trick.

There was a small stone building about the size of a telephone booth short of the drawbridge. It was a telephone booth. About fifteen seconds after I lifted the phone from its cradle, a man's voice said, "Hello."

"My name is Brock Callahan," I said, "and I meant to phone Mr. Allingham from San Valdesto last night but learned he had an unlisted number. I would like to speak with him about a personal matter."

"That name again, please."

"Brock Callahan. He might remember who I am. I used to play football for the Los Angeles Rams."

"One moment, please."

Less than a minute later, I could hear the grinding sound of the drawbridge lowering as the voice said, "Mr. Allingham will see you."

The iron-plated portcullis was already lifting when I drove over the drawbridge. Cyrus ran a tight ship.

He was standing on the top stone step in front of his heavy double doors as I walked over from my car. He was thin and tall, dressed in gray flannel trousers and a short-sleeved white cotton shirt. He was smiling.

"The Rock," he said. "It has been some time since I've seen you in action. Do you miss it?"

His hand was bony, his grip strong. I shook my head. "Not much. Nice little place you have here. I wish I could afford one like it."

He smiled again. "Come in."

To the right of the entry hall, an immense two-story living room was furnished in a décor only two or three centuries closer to the modern mode than the castle.

He indicated a tapestried armchair near the front windows, and I sat down. I asked, "Who designed this place for you?"

"I did most of the designing," he told me. "Of course, I had an architectural consultant. But I'm sure you didn't drive all the way from San Valdesto just to see the house."

"No. But I've been investing rather heavily in gold lately, and I'm beginning to believe I might need a place like this, the way things are going in our country."

He nodded. "I heard about your inheritance from your uncle.

I knew your Uncle Homer. We sold him most of his oil-drilling equipment."

"He died at the right time," I said, "for him and for me. When my Aunt Sheila divorced him, he had no more reason to live. And he wouldn't have understood what's going on in our country today."

"Who does?" he said. "Well, about the house, I studied the work of a French designer named Sebastian le Prestre de Vauban before I started work on this place. He was the master of fortification. And also, I might add, of siegecraft. I added some minor innovations of my own. Vauban had water in his moats. My moat is mined."

"Uncle Homer had water in his," I said. I paused to study him, then said, "You will probably think I'm being intrusive, but I came up here to talk about your former son-in-law."

"Go on," he said quietly.

"He phoned me," I said, "shortly after he came to San Valdesto. I guess he assumed I was still a private investigator. I was annoyed by his call and told him so. When I was still in my second year with the Rams, he tried to cheat me out of five thousand dollars. I had to threaten him with physical violence to get my money back."

His smile was thin. "I wish I had. Go on."

"A few nights after that, I was in a poker game with several of the police officers I know in San Valdesto. I overheard some remarks that led me to believe that Baker is...threatening you. Is that right?"

"It is. Have you decided to go back into investigative work?"

"Not for pay," I said. "But if there is any way I can be of help, I want to volunteer my services. Not that I'm vindictive, I hope you understand, but —" I smiled. "We Ram fans must stick together. And I don't want the ideals you represent to be besmirched by a foul ball like Alan Arthur Baker."

"Thank you," he said quietly. "Thank you very much. If I need your help, I will certainly call on you. But I think my present problem with Alan will soon be resolved. You could call it the fight-fire-with-fire technique. He won't get another dime out of me."

"Good," I said. "May I intrude with one more suggestion?"

"Of course."

"I hope," I said, "that you are not being represented in San Valdesto by Joe Farini. He has a reputation of being unreliable. He could double-cross you."

He shook his head. "He represents Alan. But thank you for the information. It could be useful. Even buying a crooked lawyer could cost less than Alan." He stood up. "I'd like to ask you to stay for lunch, Brock, but I have another appointment in ten minutes."

I went out without seeing Luther's cousin. The butler held the door open for me. The portcullis closed behind me as I drove over the drawbridge, and the drawbridge lifted as I reached the other side of the moat. The precise mechanics of today's science are awesome.

At the far end of the long driveway, a gray car was just turning in off the road. This must be the appointment Allingham had mentioned.

I stopped my car, got out, and lifted the hood. When the gray car, a Volvo, drew abreast, I had the dip stick in my hand and was examining it.

"Trouble?" the driver of the Volvo called.

"My oil-pressure needle was quivering," I explained, "and I wanted to check the level."

I turned around—and saw the beefy, red face of Max Kronen. Max ran a fairly large investigative office in the San Fernando Valley.

"Callahan," he said. "What are you doing here?"

"You first," I said.

"Come on, muscles! You're retired. I'm not."

"Ask Mr. Allingham," I advised him.

"I'll not only ask him," he said. "I'll warn him."

He went into the stone phone booth; I put the dip stick back into its socket. I was almost out of the long driveway when he left the booth.

Fight fire with fire, Allingham had said. He wasn't going to pay Alan another dime. That could mean he had uncovered something that he could trade, some counterblackmail on Alan. Or maybe on Felicia? That might be the link where the cases were connected.

The flabby brawn of Maximillian Kronen against the wily brain of Alan Arthur Baker? That should make an interesting confrontation.

It was still short of noon and I was going down the coast road. I decided to take the Donegal Bay exit and learn if dapper Duane Detterwald had sold another ranch. Or could tell me about that party at the Kratzerts'.

He was in the office, talking on the phone, when I entered. He glared at me and said, "Something has come up, Marilyn. I'll call you back as soon as I'm free."

When he hung up, I asked, "The redhead?"

He nodded curtly. "You are one lying bastard, aren't you?"

"At times," I admitted. "What's bugging you now?"

"That phony story about looking for your young friend. You were checking on Mike."

"I was not. I was looking for my friend. He was here; he even ate at Mike's place, but he wasn't checking on him either. What's got you so hot?"

He didn't answer.

"Something has happened. Speak up."

He said, "There was another peeper here asking about Mike, a guy named Max Kronen. Are you working with him?"

"I am not, nor would I. I talked with him about a half an hour ago, though, up in Veronica Village. He had an appointment with the man I had gone to see, a man named Cyrus Allingham. Do you know him?"

"That Nazi creep? Only by name. Is he mixed up in this, too?"

"I don't know. This I do know—your friend Mike's old girl

friend might be involved with him through her husband. I am speaking of Felicia Baker, the former Felicia Rowan."

"Who told you she's Mike's old girl friend?"

"My wife. Mike brought Mrs. Baker to a party at her house before we were married. You might remember my wife. Her name was Jan Bonnet when you went to high school with her."

He stared at me. "You married Jan Bonnet? How come you didn't mention it when you were up here before?"

"I saw no reason to."

He shook his head. "A doll like that? You? I sure expected better from her. She was one classy girl."

"She still is. Keep running me down, shorty, and earn yourself a fat lip."

He picked up a brass letter opener from his desk and glared at me again. "Take your best shot, King Kong, and then I'll open your jugular."

I started to laugh. When he came around the desk, the needle-pointed opener still in his hand, I stopped laughing. "Duane," I said quietly, "put it down. You know you're not going to use it. I'm almost sure we're on the same side in this mess. Believe me!"

There was some doubt in his glare now.

"All right," he said finally, "but lay off that shorty crap."

"I apologize. Remember, though, you took some shots at me. Is there any place besides Mike's where we can have lunch? I don't want him to see us together."

"Mike's is the only place in town," he told me. "But he won't be there. He's out fishing today. My nephew's girl friend is working the kitchen. She's great with fish. We can have that."

The Rusty Anchor was busier that day than at my first visit. About two-thirds of the tables in the room were occupied, and two more diners were eating at the bar.

"Don't order the clam chowder," Duane said. "Mike makes that. In clam country, he uses canned clams."

"I know," I said. "I've had it."

We sat at a small, round table in a corner of the room. How much, I wondered, could I confide in Duane Detterwald?

A thin, middle-aged waitress in jeans and a flowered blouse took our order. We ordered a pitcher of Einlicher and the broiled red snapper and rye rolls.

As I poured our beer, I asked, "Do you know Felicia Baker?"

He nodded. "She stayed at our house a few nights ago. I introduced her to Mike. The title to this place is in her name."

"Mike told me it was his place. He told me he bought it from his cousin."

"He did. He bought it from his cousin with money he got from Felicia. She wanted to give it to him. I nixed that. Mike would have sold the place and taken off. It's his, rent-free, as long as he runs it. All the profits are his."

"You nixed it? I thought Mike was your buddy."

"He is. But that's emotional, right? Who should understand that better than you? Mike is a bum. If it wasn't for his fists, he would have been a vagrant. Felicia and I know that."

"Are Mike and Felicia still friends?"

He shook his head. "With Mike, women are lays, not people. Felicia steers clear of him now that she's married."

New patterns were forming, a new scenario was building in my mind. *Slow down*, I told myself.

Duane ran a forefinger slowly around the rim of his beaker. He didn't look at me as he said, "I'm getting a picture."

I said nothing.

He looked up at me. "This young peeper friend of yours, he was checking out Felicia for her husband, wasn't he? Her husband thinks she's still hot for Mike. You can tell him to forget it."

I continued to say nothing.

"I owe Mike," he said. "Since high school, I owe Mike. He protected me from the kind of guys who use words like 'midget.'"

"Or 'weasel,'" I said.

He smiled. "Jan told you that, didn't she?"

I nodded. "I'm sorry I called you 'shorty.'"

"And I'm sorry," he told me, "that I said you weren't good enough for Jan. You almost are."

Our red snapper came then, along with the rye rolls—plus cole slaw, compliments of the house for Uncle Duane.

"Your nephew," I told Duane, "is even dumber than Mike is if he doesn't marry this girl. This is tops!"

"Marry? Today's kids?" He snorted. "They're all Mikes today—rootless, careless drifters."

Duane Detterwald was my kind of man, if my instincts were sound. Unfortunately, my instincts are not always sound.

Chapter Eight

WHEN we parted, I told Duane to drop in any time he was down our way. He and Jan could reminisce about their high-school days.

"My high-school memories aren't that pleasant," he said, "but looking at Jan again would make the trip worthwhile. You treat her right, Callahan, or you'll answer to me."

"I will. And you keep an eye on Mike. If Cyrus Reed Allingham is out to get him, Mike could be in more trouble than he can handle."

"Mike has always been in more trouble than he can handle. At least outside of the ring. If you learn anything—"

"I'll phone you. Give my love to Marilyn."

He laughed. "We finally got an offer on that house, two hundred and thirty-two thousand. That's what three-bedroom, two-bath fixer-uppers are going for in Donegal Valley. She asked me half a dozen times when you were coming back to make an offer. I told her you were waiting for an offer on your Brentwood home before you made a decision on hers."

Realtors—they're almost as tricky as private eyes....

Up the steep and winding road the Mustang moved, past the houses on the bluff and down into the valley. Felicia's lie was still a lie; she knew what Mike was doing now, even if she didn't see him. Why would she lie about it?

Possibly because her husband had been in the room when I asked her. He must have known her history, traveling in the circles he did. And she must know he knew. So why the secrecy, so long as she was innocent (to use the word loosely)?

There was a slight breeze from the ocean, and the sun's glare was softened by stationary cumulus clouds. It was a day for golf, but here I was, back on the prowl. When would I join the leisure class Uncle Homer had made possible for me? Not until I ran out of more interesting things to do.

I had shaken the hand of Cyrus Reed Allingham. I had pretended to share his views. I had avoided the final ignominy; I had not asked for his autograph.

Faith was what Cyrus was selling, faith in the time-honored American values and traditions. Time had not exactly honored many of our traditions. Among them are slavery, killing Indians, civil war, denying women the right to vote, child labor, depletion of our natural resources, and a still-virulent bigotry.

Faith may be wonderful, as some cynical sage has pointed out, but it is doubt that will get you an education. I would have to stay committed to the immoral minority. To camouflage that, I was forced to remain devious.

When I came home, Mrs. Casey informed me that Lieutenant Vogel had phoned and asked that I call him back. I got him at the station.

"When you were working down in L.A.," he asked me, "did you ever run into a private investigator named Max Kronen?"

"Occasionally. As a matter of fact, I talked with him only a couple of hours ago. Why do you ask?"

"You mean he came up here to see *you?*"

"Answer my question first."

"I was hoping that you might give me a line on his reputation. He could be working for Joe Farini."

"Are you still watching Joe?"

"Yes. Your turn."

"I was leaving Cyrus Allingham's wigwam up in Veronica Village this morning when Max drove in. My hunch is that he's working for Allingham."

"What reason did you have to visit Cyrus Allingham?"

"I was obeying the instructions you gave me in your office yesterday afternoon."

"I never gave you any such instructions!"

"Your memory is weak. You told me to keep you informed. You wished me good hunting."

"All right, all right! What did you learn up there?"

"I learned that a French engineer named Vauban was the acknowledged master of fortification and siegecraft. I've forgotten his first names. He had a lot of 'em."

"Damn you! Talk sense."

"Bernie," I said soothingly, "it is almost the cocktail hour. Why don't you stop in here before you go home, and we'll have a quiet talk and a strong drink?"

"All right," he said for the third time, this time less heatedly.

On a piece of graph paper I put down the names of all the people I had talked with since Baker had phoned me. I drew lines between the obvious connections and tried to find a pattern in them. The only pattern I could find was what Allingham called it — fighting fire with fire. It shaped up as a blackmail standoff.

But what could Allingham know about the Bakers that was not common knowledge? She had been a hooker, he a con man; Allingham could have learned that from the public press. He obviously had needed more than that. So he had hired Max Kronen to get it for him. Max must have come up with something, or at least convinced Cyrus that he had.

Alan had been privy to more knowledge of the Allingham family than the press was likely to learn — or to print. Cyrus had friends in high places. He had zealous, vindictive supporters in high, medium, and low places. Anyone who dared to defame him would need to be armed with more than hearsay evidence.

When Jan came home, I told her Bernie would be stopping in for a drink.

"And a yack fest about skulduggery," she added. "I'll take my shower while you two get that over with, and join you later for more civilized conversation."

"For your sadly thin information, madame," I informed her,

"Bernie and I are the citizen types who help to keep the world civilized."

"Orderly, maybe," she said. "I will not accept civilized." She patted my cheek. Each to his own, Lochinvar. Charge!"

"Smartass," I said, and kissed her.

Bernie's car pulled into our driveway about five minutes later. I knew what he wanted—Scotch over rocks. I had it waiting for him when he reached our front door.

He studied me suspiciously.

"I am trying to play the gracious host," I explained. "Don't just stand there. We have important matters to discuss."

We went out in back, and I gave him the account of my day, from the Allingham fortress to Donegal Bay.

"That's all out of my jurisdiction," he said.

"I know. That's what I've been wondering about."

"What do you mean by that?"

"The Bakers don't live in the city, either. They're out of your jurisdiction, too. The only one involved in this mess who isn't outside is Joe Farini. What is this, a police vendetta?"

"Easy, now," he said quietly.

"Maybe," I suggested, "some of the boys down there want to pay Luther back by nailing Farini."

He shook his head. "Your mouth is ahead of your brain, as usual. I'll admit we want to get something on Farini. We don't like crooked lawyers. And the state Bar Association hasn't done a damned thing about him. Tell me, self-ordained knight in tarnished armor, do you like crooked lawyers?"

I stared at him admiringly. "That's *great*—self-ordained knight in tarnished armor. Is it a quote?"

"Oh, shut up!" he said.

"It has earned you another drink," I told him, and took his glass.

Jan was there when I brought his drink. I went to get her a gin and tonic, and fortified my own glass.

"Now," Bernie said, "tell me what you know about Max Kronen."

I said, "I know that he almost lost his license about three years ago for beating up a stoolie who had double-crossed him. I never followed his career. The other boys in the trade consider him more brawn than brain."

"Which is not unusual in your trade."

"Thank you!"

"I meant, of course," he explained, "the *other* boys in your trade. Does he have a specialty? Divorce, industrial spying— what?"

"I doubt it. He has four investigators working for him, three men and one woman. They might specialize. My peers have told me he has a real fancy office down there in the San Fernando Valley. And he has worked for some high-priced lawyers. I got the impression they have him on a retainer basis."

"Criminal lawyers?"

"Not all of them. The only one I can think of is Norman Geller."

"Norman Geller," Vogel said, "is married to Farini's sister. They shared an office up here for a couple of years."

"There is your connection," I said. "Now Jan would like to have some civilized conversation."

They stayed with the literary B's that day—Barthelme, Borges, and Bellow. I had to wait until they got to Bellow to worm my way into the conversation.

Bernie left, we had dinner, the sun went down. There was nothing but garbage, as usual, on the commercial tube. PBS was offering us a string quartet playing one of the musical B's, Brahms. Jan listened to that. I phoned the Raleigh house, and Corey was home.

"What's new?" I asked him.

"Nothing exciting. Do you know a man named Max Kronen?"

"I do. Why?"

"He came to my house this afternoon and tried to question my dad about me. My dad told him to get lost."

"You watch out for him, Corey. He could be a rough customer."

"Not as rough as my dad. What is he, a private eye?"

"He is. And it's possible he's working for Joe Farini. Lieutenant Vogel was here before dinner, asking about him."

"How come he asked you? Are you getting into this case?"

"Not your end of it. But I have a gut feeling that you'll be calling on me before long. Did Mrs. Baker leave the house today?"

"Oh, yes! She went to the beauty parlor to have her hair tinted and then to the Biltmore for lunch and then to I. Magnin for some shopping and then home. Dullsville! Who needs a Sam Spade for that kind of surveillance?"

"Corey, you are not Sam Spade. You be careful!"

"Yes, sir," he said. "Of course, sir. Keep in touch, teach."

He was getting too big for his britches. Kids. I went in and listened to Brahms with Jan.

It was a troubled night of confused dreams dimly remembered. My father was mixed up in it somehow, and the Hearst Castle and the party at Jan's house in Beverly Glen, the party where Mike Anthony had brought Felicia Rowan. One of these days I would have to hit the couch to see if a shrink could make any sense out of my dreams.

"You were muttering again," Jan said in the morning. "Bad night?"

"Too many dreams. Who said 'the stuff that dreams are made of'?"

"Sam Spade in *The Maltese Falcon*. Shakespeare said it better in *The Tempest* — 'We are such stuff as dreams are made on, and our little life is rounded with a sleep.'"

"I guess Hammett was no Shakespeare, huh?"

She shrugged. "Hammett edged him in plotting. Would you like waffles for breakfast, master?"

"Great! And some of those tasty pork sausages you bought in Solvang. How come you didn't go to college?"

"I couldn't play football," she explained, "and I didn't want to blunt my education."

Orange juice, waffles with pork sausage, coffee with the *Los Angeles Times*. The morning was overcast; it would clear before noon along the coast, which is where we lived.

I was reading the stock quotations to find out how much money I had lost yesterday when Mrs. Casey came in to tell me Lieutenant Vogel was on the phone.

"Don't come rushing down here," he warned me, "but I thought I should inform you."

"Down where?"

"To the Travis Hotel. Luther Barnum has been murdered."

Chapter Nine

"WHY shouldn't I come down? I won't get in your way."

"I'm sure you wouldn't. But there are other officers here, and I would prefer to not let them know you have more cooperation from the department than some of *their* investigator friends."

"I get it. Any suspects?"

"We'll talk about that in my office. I should be back there by eleven o'clock, at the latest."

When I came back to the breakfast room, Jan asked, "What now?"

"A man has been murdered—Luther Barnum, a police stoolie." I sat down and picked up the *Times*.

"Is he involved in this—this business with Alan Baker?"

"Maybe."

"Don't act so bored, Sherlock. You are itching to get down there. Admit it."

"I'm going down later to talk with Bernie about it in his office. I'm not bored; I'm depressed. A gutsy little old man has just been murdered."

"I'm sorry I was flippant. Did you know him?"

"Briefly. Let's talk about something else."

She went to work half an hour later. I sat. Could it have been Max Kronen? He had beaten up a stoolie. Or Mr. Five-by-five? He had threatened Luther. Had he been stabbed, throttled, shot, bludgeoned? That was the least Bernie could have told me.

At ten o'clock, I figured the law would have deserted the premises by now. I drove down to the Travis Hotel.

The same clerk was behind the counter, wearing the same shiny blue serge trousers. He had replaced the clean white shirt with a clean blue work shirt.

"I was in here a couple of days ago to see Luther Barnum," I said, "and I just learned about—about what happened."

He nodded. "I remember your visit, Mr. Callahan."

"You know me?"

He smiled. "Of course. I watched you play many times when I lived in Los Angeles. Was Luther a friend of yours?"

"Not really. But I was wondering—is anybody going to pay for the funeral? Does he have relatives?"

"A cousin," he told me. "She lives up in Veronica Village. Our manager has already notified her."

"When did it happen?"

"Sometime last night. I wasn't on duty. The night clerk is down at the station being questioned by the police right now."

"How was he killed?"

"Poisoned liquor. Somebody must have brought it to his room. He never left the hotel yesterday."

"Oh God!" I said. "I brought him a bottle when I came."

"I know. I saw the bottle. That was whiskey. This was cognac. The bottle was still in his room."

It was still short of eleven o'clock when I got to the station, but Bernie was in his office. So were Captain Dahl and a uniformed officer. I waited in the hall until they left.

Bernie looked up from behind his desk as I came in. "We're waiting for a lab report," he told me. "The paramedics who answered the call believe he was poisoned, but they're not doctors."

"Any solid suspects?"

He shook his head. "The night clerk said that if anybody went to Luther's room, he didn't stop at the desk first. That figures. It isn't likely that the killer would announce himself."

"I hope he isn't going to be buried in a pauper's grave."

"He isn't. The manager of the hotel said Luther's cousin up there in Veronica Village enrolled Luther in that nonprofit memorial society in town here almost a year ago. There'll be no funeral, so she won't be coming down. He'll be cremated." He stood up and arched his back and rubbed his neck. "Are you thinking what I'm thinking—that Farini's fine hand is involved in this?"

"No. Not in murder. Even the Bar Association wouldn't stand still for murder. Joe couldn't take the chance of hiring somebody who might be linked to him later."

Bernie said wearily, "You're probably right. Just the same, we're going to interrogate Kronen and that Rafferty freak."

"Who is the Rafferty freak?"

"That Farini stooge you decked. He threatened Luther, didn't he, while you were in the room?"

"Not quite. All he said to Luther was 'Who you squeaking to now'? The rest of his remarks were directed at me."

"We'll grill him anyway. And Kronen has beat up a stoolie before. We'll sweat him, too."

The lab report came in a few minutes later. The cognac had been laced with strychnine. Death by poisoning was the verdict. A man with Max's connections might be able to buy strychnine at some pest-control store that didn't require certification of its use. But he wouldn't have added it to cognac. He had the reputation of keeping a sharp eye on expenses. And he had the experience to know that the Luther Barnum type would prefer fortified wine or blended corn.

I said, "We still can't be sure who Max is working for, can we? We assumed he's working for Farini because he *might* be on retainer to Farini's brother-in-law. Up in Veronica Village I had to assume he was working for Allingham, because he had an appointment with him."

"We'll find out when we sweat him."

"I doubt it. That is privileged information, and I'm sure Max knows it. But think of this—Max has no loyalty, except to the dollar, and Farini is famous as a double-cross artist."

"Do you think Max could be playing double agent?"

"Farini is clever enough to have an agent in the enemy camp.

And Max would sell out to the highest bidder. That makes him a logical choice for a double agent."

Bernie yawned. "Tricky, isn't it? It would take a trickier mind than mine to decipher it."

"That is certainly true," I agreed. "Well, I've got a date for golf this afternoon and I haven't had lunch yet. See you around, Bernie."

"Buddy!" he said.

"Don't 'buddy' me," I told him. "You never make it official. You and your damned hints, which you can deny making later to protect your own skin. Well, I have skin, too."

"I've noticed," he said. "And it's so *thin!* How can it keep all that muscle from bursting through it?"

"Luck," I said, and walked out, waiting for him to call me back.

He didn't. That sly fox knew me. Or thought he did. I could change. I'd show him.

It was chance that brought me back to my former attitude. I was tooling along the freeway, heading for home, when I happened to notice this gray Volvo in front of me. There are a lot of those. This one bore the insignia of a San Fernando Valley car dealer on the frame around the license plate. There are more than a few of those, too.

But, two cars ahead, another gray car — an old Plymouth — was also cruising in the righthand lane. It looked like Corey's car. I passed the Volvo and cut sharply back in front of it. The driver tooted his horn. I slowed down. When he tried to go around me, I moved over to block him. He leaned on his horn. I waved at him. It was Max.

Ahead, the gray Plymouth was taking the Lobero exit. I followed it, and the Volvo followed me. It was Corey's car ahead; I could see the broken lens in the right taillight.

No traffic had followed us onto the ramp. Halfway up it, I cut over to the middle, as Corey's car turned north on Lobero and headed for the hills.

I hit the brakes and heard the screech of the Volvo's tires

from behind. I waved for Max to pull over on the flat stretch of grass to the right of the ramp. When he did, I pulled over in front of him and got out of my car.

His jowls were quivering, his small eyes blazing. "What in hell do you think you're doing, Callahan?" he asked me.

"I'm protecting my young friend," I said. "You were following Corey Raleigh."

"So what? What makes it your business?"

"Max," I said, "this is kind of an insular little town that Corey and I live in, and the police don't like private investigators from L.A. who come up and bring trouble with them. I wanted to warn you."

"No kidding? I imagine the police aren't too crazy about you, either."

"You're wrong on that. Both Corey and I have connections with the department. And his uncle, a veteran in the department, was very annoyed when he learned you had threatened Corey's father."

"That's a lot of crap. I talked with him. I never threatened him. If there were any threats, they were his. And I'll ask you again, what makes it your business?"

"Well, you see, Corey and I often work together. I trained the lad. But he doesn't have the beef you and I have, so I'm kind of his muscle man. And I remembered how you beat up that poor little stoolie three years ago."

"That stoolie," he said, "pulled a knife on me."

He put his left arm outside his car window. He was wearing a short-sleeved shirt. He showed me the long, jagged, livid scar that ran from his inner wrist all the way up to his inner elbow. He said, "He tried to kill me. Does your young friend carry a knife?"

"Not yet. Tell me, Max, are you working for Allingham or Joe Farini?"

"That's none of your damned business and you know it."

"I'm making it mine. The way I figure it, Norman Geller, Farini's brother-in-law, probably recommended you."

"You figure it any God-damned way you want, Irish. But neither you nor your cop friends have a right to ask me in this town or any other. What the hell is it with you? What's your beef with me? You weren't exactly Mr. Clean when you worked down in L.A."

"My beef is Corey Raleigh, and I've warned you. Lay off the kid."

"Drop dead," he said, and started his engine. He swung out to pull around my car, and turned north on Lobero, just as Corey had.

I, too, took Lobero, the long route home. Max pulled into a filling station about a block from the ramp. I drove on.

Corey's car was parked in front of the house when I got there. He got out of it as I drove into the driveway and met me as I got out of my car.

"Was that you," he asked, "who stopped Kronen on the Lobero exit?"

"It was. Did you know he was tailing you?"

"Of course I knew it! I was going to lead him up into the hills and get him lost. He wouldn't be able to find his way back for hours with all those crazy roads up there. God knows why he was tailing me. I'm not working today. The Bakers are in Los Angeles."

I couldn't think of anything to say.

"Were you tailing him?" Corey asked.

I shook my head. "I just happened to notice he was following you."

"And you thought I didn't know it? I saw his car down in Donegal Bay. He came to my house and tried to question my father. Why does he drive that Volvo you can spot from a mile away? Brock, I said if I needed you, I would call on you!"

I nodded humbly. "Come into the house. We'll have lunch and a beer and a talk."

Chapter Ten

THE lunch Mrs. Casey served us was a little fancier than she provided when I ate alone—beef stroganoff. Mrs. Casey thinks Corey is the cutest thing that's come along since Peter Pan.

I told him about the murder of Luther Barnum and added, "It could be involved with your case." I went on to explain my counterblackmail theory and told him about meeting Kronen in front of the Allingham castle.

"If it's that clean-cut," he said, "the Allinghams against the Bakers, why would Mr. Baker pay me to shadow his wife?"

"That's what's puzzling Lieutenant Vogel and me. It could be that he's using you more as a bodyguard than as a snoop. And we can't figure out which side Kronen is on."

"I hope he's on our side," Corey said. "I don't have the muscle to be a bodyguard."

He left right after lunch; he had to take his mother shopping. I phoned Bernie and told him about my encounter with Max Kronen. "Just so you're prepared," I said, "if he comes in and makes a complaint about me."

"I thought you were going to play golf."

"I am. In five minutes. I'm phoning from the pro shop."

He laughed. "I'll bet you are! Kronen won't have to come in of his own volition. We'll bring him in. Stay with it, citizen."

He knows me too well, that man.

Threats and counterthreats, skulduggery, chicanery, lies, and evasions.... And now murder. Luther Barnum had said that what he had told me was all he knew. Somebody must have thought he knew more. Or, possibly, Luther had learned more since my visit. Maybe somebody had offered him more money than I had. The killer certainly had brought him fancier booze.

I couldn't believe he had been a principal in the cast, only a peripheral victim. If it hadn't been for his relationship to Farini, his death would have occasioned minimal police interest. His only living relative had not traveled the forty miles from Veronica Village to arrange his funeral.

It was still early afternoon. I phoned Bernie again to learn the cousin's name, but he was not in the office. I didn't want to ask anyone else; I was not that popular at the station.

I climbed aboard my ancient steed and headed for Veronica Village. It was Friday and the weekend traffic was heavy: Los Angelenos heading for the clean air and open spaces. But we made it without strain in less than an hour.

A feminine voice answered the phone. I identified myself and said, "I'd like to speak with Mr. Allingham again. He knows me."

"My father is out of town," the voice said, "but I'll see you, Mr. Callahan."

Down with the drawbridge, up with the portcullis, back to the Middle Ages.

She met me at the door, a plain and full-bodied tall woman with eyes of dark blue. She was wearing a white linen skirt and tan blouse.

"Mrs. Baker?" I asked.

She smiled and shook her head. "Not anymore. I took back my maiden name after the divorce. My father told me of your previous visit. I'm sorry he isn't here today. Come in."

We went into the same lofty living room; I sat in the same chair I had graced before. I said, "I came up to talk with your maid, Luther Barnum's cousin."

"Why?"

"Lieutenant Vogel, a friend of mine, feels that there might be something she would know about Luther's background that could reveal a possible enemy. I've worked successfully with Lieutenant Vogel before, and he knows that many of the officers in the San Valdesto Police Department are not overly concerned with what happened to Luther. He has... quite often embarrassed them in court by giving them evidence that turned out to be false."

She frowned. "You mean he was a — a — "

"An informer," I said.

"I see. I hate to sound inhospitable after you have driven all the way up here, Mr. Callahan, but Lucy has been so distressed since her cousin's death that the doctor gave her a sedative. She's resting now. Is it possible I could be of help?"

"Perhaps. First, for background, your former husband tried to cheat me when I was a much younger and dumber man than I am now."

She nodded. "My father told me about that. Surely, though, neither you nor the police can suspect that Alan might have anything to do with — with what happened?"

"Maybe not directly, though even that is possible. Through a friend who plays cards with him, I learned that Alan and a disreputable attorney in San Valdesto have become rather close. And when I was last up here, I met a private investigator named Max Kronen who had come to see your father. Did your father hire him?"

"Definitely not! He is working for an attorney in your town, a man named Joseph Farini. Is that the disreputable attorney you mentioned?"

"That's the man. And three years ago Max Kronen almost lost his investigator's license for severely battering an informer who worked for him, and apparently double-crossed him. That, with the information your father gave me when I talked to him, might indicate that your former husband might be more than indirectly involved in Luther Barnum's murder."

"No," she said. "Not Alan. When we were divorced, my father paid him a very substantial sum of money to get him out of my life. I guess he now claims he had dug up some information about my father, some scandal my father refuses to discuss with me. From the crumbs of information I've managed to gather, it's a business scandal. My father, as I am sure you are aware, Mr. Callahan, has been pictured in the press as a ruthless business man. But not even his most vicious critics have ever claimed he was dishonest." She was shaking when she finished. She stared at the floor, breathing heavily.

I said gently, "But you still don't believe that Alan had anything to do with the murder?"

"No." Her voice was soft. "He doesn't have the — the stomach for that. You know, he is actually a very gentle man — though not really a gentleman, is he?" Her smile was sad. "I sound as if I'm still in love with him, don't I?"

"Are you?"

"No. But I can understand him, though our thinking is poles apart. I wish he could have tried harder to understand my father. With Alan's considerable gift of persuasion, he could have helped my father's cause so much!"

I stood up. "You have been very cooperative. I am sure your father's enemies will not prevail. Would it be possible for me to talk with Lucy at some later time?"

She was smiling now, the gracious lady. "Of course. I am almost sure she will, once the shock wears off. I'll find an opportune time to ask her and then phone you if she agrees."

"Thank you," I said. "Give my best to your father."

"I shall. I am sure he will regret having missed you. He was always a devoted Rams fan."

Traffic was light on the way home; the heavy traffic was on the other side of the divider. We dawdled along at fifty-five miles an hour.

If Max was working for Farini, why had he been checking on Corey? Corey was working for Baker, and so was Farini. Alan and Felicia had gone to Farini's office *together*.

The bodyguard theory I had suggested was doubtful. Corey was too fragile for that role. But Corey, I reminded myself, had not been Baker's first choice for the job. I had.

A con man, a crooked attorney, a greedy private eye; what

rational mind could decipher the machinations of minds like those? All of their loyalties were temporary, except to their mutual god—money.

About twelve miles short of San Valdesto, a jerk in a Porsche came alongside and looked over with the scornful smile those pukes reserve for drivers of shoddy Detroit vehicles.

The road ahead was clear to the horizon. I bottomed my right foot and so did he. Four miles later, the Porsche was only a tiny red dot in my rearview mirror.

Didn't the nitwit know that even the original Henry's Model T had a bigger engine than his puddle-jumper?

Vogel usually went home early on Fridays. I phoned him there when I got home. I told him I had learned it was Farini that Max was working for.

"Where did you learn that?"

"Up at Veronica Village about an hour ago."

"I thought you were going to play golf."

"Get off that tired kick! What's new at your end?"

"We have a partial print off the cognac bottle that doesn't match Luther's. What were you doing in Veronica Village?"

"I was having a conversation with Joan Allingham. Luther's cousin was resting under sedation and incommunicado. Joan thinks Baker is threatening her father with revealing some old business scandal. She also told me that Max Kronen is working for Farini. If you get a make on that print, you'll let me know, won't you?"

"Yes. Thanks for the info. Farini was in with the chief this afternoon, screaming harassment."

"Let's hope the chief doesn't buy it."

"Even if he does, we've always got you," he told me.

Another day of pretense, playing a role of somebody I wasn't. Cyrus would probably send my name to his multifarious mailing lists. Our mailbox would be flooded with the super-WASP, superpatriot idiocies those organizations considered to be the only acceptable Americanism.

I had nobody to blame but myself; I could have played golf.

"Down?" Jan asked when she came home.

"A little. You don't look too up, yourself."

"Tedium," she said. "Trivia. Chasing a dollar I don't need."

"There is one thing we must not forget," I pointed out. "We were even more bored before we went back to work."

I was adding today's revelations to my journal when the phone rang.

It was Duane Detterwald. He was phoning from the Biltmore Hotel in town. Would it be possible, he asked, for Jan and me to join him and his wife for dinner there tonight?

When I asked Jan, she said, "Tell them to come here. We have a leg of lamb and there'll be plenty for all. Duane will pep us up. He was always a positive thinker."

They came early enough for a drink. Duane had done well by himself; his wife, Daphne, was a pert and sassy imitation blonde only a few inches taller that he was.

She made points with Jan the moment she entered the living room. She looked around and sighed. "This is what I have always wanted, a house decorated by Jan Bonnet! But I suppose you're retired now?"

"Not yet," Jan said. "Let me show you the other rooms."

They left, and it was Duane's turn to sigh.

"Don't fret," I said soothingly. "For an old friend like you, Jan will probably cut her markup to a hundred percent. And you can always sell another ranch. Drink?"

"Scotch on the rocks," he said.

He was sitting on the couch when I brought his drink. I asked, "Why the Biltmore? I should think you would stay with the Bakers when you came to town."

"Daphne can't stand Alan," he explained, "and neither can I. What's going on, Brock?"

I sat down next to him. "I wish I knew. My first thought was that Baker was having Felicia followed because he was jealous of Mike. But then Cyrus Allingham got mixed up in it, and Luther Barnum was murdered here in town, and—"

"That man who was murdered? How does he tie in?"

"His cousin is a maid at the Allinghams'. And I guess you know that Baker was married to Joan Allingham."

He nodded. "And now Felicia's worried about Mike but won't confide in me. She might be seeing Mike on the sly. I'm going to check *that* out!"

"Let me know what you learn."

"I sure as hell will. You're one man I can trust." He laughed. "Greg Hudson! You're like me, Brock. You're too dumb to be crooked."

Chapter Eleven

It was a soul-restoring evening, trivia without tedium. Duane related the complicated handicapping system that he and a friend with access to a computer had worked out during his gambling days. It was too sophisticated for me to understand all of it. Apparently, it had also been too sophisticated for the computer. They ran their original kitty of eighteen thousand dollars down to nothing in sixteen days of racing.

Daphne related the comic joys and transient sorrows of her brief career as an exotic dancer at a less-than-exclusive nightclub called Beauty In The Buff, in Hollywood's shadowland.

When they left, Jan said, "Duane and Daphne Detterwald — do you think it was alliteration that brought them together?"

"Maybe. Whatever it was, it was certainly lucky for both of them. They belong together."

"They do. They are both darlings. We belong together, too, don't we, Brock?"

"There's a way to find out," I suggested.

"I know. Grappling. Let's go!"

A happy finish to a disspiriting day. No dreams that night, no tossing, no turning. Jan worked on Saturdays; she was gone when I woke up.

The previous evening's edition of the local paper had carried three paragraphs on the death of Luther Barnum. The morning's *Times* held no mention of it. Unmourned and little noticed — thus ended the undistinguished life of Luther Barnum.

At ten o'clock I went to the club to play with the foursome I had been neglecting. They made me pay for my unauthorized absence and lack of practice. Camaraderie *but not compassion*, that is the creed of the devout golfer.

In a mixed foursome on Sunday, I fared better. Jan helped me to get some of my money back, suggesting a press to our opponents on the short holes she knew she could handle, not suggesting it on the long holes she knew I would blow.

We topped the day with an Alan Alda movie and awakened on Monday morning ready for the real world again.

On the phone, after breakfast, Bernie told me the approximate time of death had been between eleven o'clock and midnight. The night clerk had seen no stranger go up the stairs at that time. "But," he added, "there is also a back stairway that goes to the second floor. Those are the stairs that the resident hookers use."

"How about the fingerprint?"

"Nothing yet. We sent copies to Washington and Sacramento. We should hear soon. The chief put a stop to our surveillance on Farini. Are you busy?"

"Too busy for that kind of peon labor. Duane was at our house last night. He thinks that Felicia Baker might be messing around with a former boyfriend in Donegal Bay. He's going to check it out."

"Information which you will relay to me, of course."

It was outside his jurisdiction, but I decided not to mention that. I said, "Of course."

I went back to finish reading the paper, but I couldn't concentrate. There was another resident of the Travis Hotel I knew who might have more information on the life and death of Luther Barnum than was stored in the police department files. His name was Wallace Stanton, but on lower Main Street he was known as The Judge.

It was ten o'clock now; he wouldn't be at the hotel. He would be holding court at Rubio's Rendezvous.

Rubio's was a narrow bar between a deserted former pawnshop and an active massage parlor on Front Street, half a block north of lower Main Street. Only Rubio, The Judge, and a small, thin dozing man at one of the tables in the room were in attendance when I entered.

Stanton sat at the bar, wearing his funereal black suit and white shirt and string tie. His enormous buttocks sagged over the edges of the steel stool.

"The footballer!" he greeted me.

Rubio held out a hand across the bar. "Pancho! It's been a long time, amigo."

I shook his hand and said, "I just thought I'd come down and buy you boys a drink."

The Judge smiled. "I'll have cognac."

Rubio scowled. "That was not funny!"

"I know," Stanton admitted. "But that's why he's down here." He looked at me. "Isn't it?"

"It is."

"Was Luther a friend of yours?"

I shook my head.

"Then why are you down here?"

"Because he's dead. I apologize for the intrusion." I turned toward the door.

"Wait!" Rubio said. "This is *my* place, and you are not intruding."

"I apologize, too," Stanton said. "But it annoyed me, that part about coming down just to buy us a drink. Why would you need to be phony with us?"

I said, "It must be a hangover from those days when I needed to be phony."

"Sit," he said, "and we'll talk. Rubio and I have been discussing the case. I'll have a small glass of ale."

"I'll have the same," I said.

Rubio had coffee. I sat on the stool next to The Judge.

He said, "The way we see it, the killer could not have gone up those front steps. The night clerk is very watchful about more than one person sleeping in a room where the occupant is paying single-room rates. He knows all the tenants."

He took a sip of ale. "The killer must have used the back

stairs, which serve only the second floor. The rooms on the second floor are restricted to tenants the manager has learned to trust." He paused. "Four of the rooms on that floor are occupied by the girls for their commercial purposes. They are the unofficial guardians of the back door and the back stairs."

"They could have been working in their rooms when the killer came in," I pointed out.

"All four at the same time?" The Judge shook his head. "Their business isn't that good. They are street solicitors with a few steady customers. When they are working the street, they stay close to the door. That's where their customers know they can find them."

"You two think some john went up to a girl's room. And after their business was consummated and the girl was dressing again, the john went down the hall to Luther's room?"

"It's a possibility."

"The coroner thinks he died around midnight. Would Luther open his door to a stranger that late at night?"

The Judge shrugged. "That bothers us, too. Maybe he had a bottle of his own to finish first. He could have been awake. He sleeps a lot during the day. We don't know how long it takes for strychnine to act."

"Do you have a prime suspect?" I asked.

"Not prime. Maybe choice. Somebody working for Joe Farini. Farini can afford cognac."

"No," I said. "He wouldn't take the chance. He couldn't trust his man to stay bought if he got caught. And he certainly wouldn't take the chance on his own."

Stanton said, "A doubtful rumor, hearsay. For what it's worth, one of the girls said a friend of hers had a customer who paid but didn't perform that night. It's not the first time that's happened, probably. What does it mean? Nothing."

"Did the girl name the girl who was rejected?"

The Judge looked at Rubio. Rubio frowned.

"I won't pressure her," I promised. "I'll walk softly. It could be a lead."

"A lead for the police," Rubio said. "We don't want her harassed by the police."

"I swear to you that it will stay our secret."

They looked at each other again. Then Rubio said, "Her name is Maria Lopez."

I thanked them, put a bill on the bar, and went out. The hotel was only a few blocks from here. I left my car where it was and walked over.

The clerk behind the desk was back to his white shirt with the blue trousers. I asked, "Is Maria Lopez in?"

He looked shocked. "Mr. Callahan, not you!"

"It's not what you think," I told him. "I only want to talk with her. She might know something that will help us find Luther's murderer."

"She's probably still sleeping," he said, "and I doubt that you'll find her cooperative. It's room two-eighteen."

It was close to Luther's room, on the other side of the corridor. I knocked on the door. No answer. I knocked louder.

"What's your hurry?" a feminine voice asked from the room. "I was sleeping."

The door opened. A buxom woman with deep brown eyes and a pocked olive complexion scowled out at me. She was wearing a yellow silk robe. "It's early, man!"

"I'm not here for business," I explained. "Rubio gave me your name. You can phone him if you don't believe me."

"You a cop?"

"Would Rubio give your name to a cop?"

She studied me doubtfully. I held up a ten-dollar bill.

She took it. "Come in," she said.

The room smelled of dry rot and cheap perfume. The bed was gilded, as were both chairs and the dresser.

I stood near the closed door. "I've been hired to investigate the death of Luther Barnum. My client doesn't believe the police will give it the time it deserves."

"They won't," she said. "I hope you get the son of a bitch!

91

All the girls liked Luther. We used to give him freebies. But I got no idea who would kill him."

"You might know without knowing," I said. "That man who paid you but didn't perform, that could have been a trick to get him up here."

Her chin lifted. "Who told you about that?"

I didn't answer.

"Rubio," she said. "He'll hear from me!"

"Please, Miss Lopez!" I said. "Believe me, all of us want to find out who killed Luther. Was he a big man? Did he tell you anything about himself? Was he white? Tall or short?"

"He was no talker," she told me. "I think he was dumb. You know, not in the head but — what's that word?"

"A mute?"

"That's it. He handed me a twenty and we went up. I'm getting ready for him, and the jerk turns around and walks out. He was white. He weighed maybe hundred and thirty or forty pounds, stood about five feet eight or nine inches tall."

"Did you hear him knock on any other door up here, maybe Luther's?"

She shook her head. "If it was Luther's, he wouldn't need to knock. He kept his door unlocked in case one of the girls wanted to drop in for a snort of booze and he might get some action."

"And there's nothing else you can tell me?"

She frowned. "Wait, yeh, one more thing. There was a bulge under this field jacket he was wearing." She stared at me. "You think maybe that could have been the bottle?"

"I hope we find out," I said. "Incidentally, I like the way you brightened up this room."

She smiled. "I painted the furniture myself. It's got real gold dust in it. With my age and weight, I figure I owe my johns something extra. So I give 'em a touch of class."

I went to the station from there to learn if the fingerprint had been identified. Bernie shook his head. "We got the answer from the feds and Sacramento this morning. No luck."

I told him about the Rubio-Stanton joint judgment that the

killer must have gone up the back stairs because the clerk watched the front stairs so closely for freeloaders.

"We figured the same. He went up the hustler's stairs."

I didn't break my sworn oath, but I said, "A john could go up and leave the girl's room while she was dressing again and then hit Luther."

"Maybe, but how many of their customers have names?"

"That's true. Are you hungry? I'll buy you a lunch."

"I thought you'd never ask," he said.

Chapter Twelve

OVER lox, bagels, and cream cheese at Plotkin's Pantry, I told Bernie, "I think the man we're looking for is white, weighs about a hundred and thirty-five pounds, stands five feet eight and a half inches tall, doesn't talk much, might even be a mute. He was wearing a field jacket."

He stared at me. "Where did you learn all that?"

"From bits and pieces. From a number of my informants."

"Don't bull me, Johnny-come-lately! We have ten times as many informants as you have."

"But they don't always confide in you boys, Bernie. That is all I am going to tell you and all that I know."

"It's a big help," he said scornfully. "There can't be more than a couple of thousand men that size and weight in town. Have you considered the possibility that a *trained* interrogator might get more out of this source than you did?"

"I said it was a number of informants, not one."

"I know you did. But you were lying."

"That's my edge," I admitted. "I don't have your official clout, so I have to lie. And it often gets me answers from people who wouldn't tell you the time of day."

"All right," he said. "All right! But I still think it's a dirty way to work."

"We're in a dirty business, Bernie. Let's have another beer."

He went back to the station from there. I went home. Maybe we had a "how" now, but not a "who" or a "why." Farini would know about those guardians of the back door. They were his clients. They could be beholden to him, willing to lie for him.

And he wouldn't have needed to use one of his local thugs; he could have hired a professional hit man from out of town.

But pros don't leave prints behind.

I was working out with the weights when that casual remark of Luther's came back to me: "I think I know why, but that's a different story."

I went in to phone the Baker house. Alan answered. I told him, "I'm working with Lieutenant Vogel on the Luther Barnum murder. I talked with Luther a few days before he died, and he said something that's puzzling me. Could I come over and talk with you?"

"Not this afternoon. I'm due downtown in twenty minutes. Couldn't we talk over the phone?"

"Okay. The way I see it, the boys in the department would love to pin this murder on one of Farini's stooges, but I don't see it that way."

"Neither do I. Go on."

"I guess you know Luther was a cousin of a maid you once employed."

"I do. Lucy Barnum. A very winsome wench. So?"

"Luther told me that he knew why Lucy stayed with Joan after the divorce, but that, he told me, was a different story."

"Why wouldn't she stay with Joan? Joan hired her."

"Is that the only reason, Alan?"

"It's the main reason. Lucy had this idea I lusted for her. I'll admit maybe I did. But I never made a serious pass at her, just a friendly pat on the rump now and then. When I saw it wasn't getting me anywhere, I quit it. What the hell does that have to do with the murder?"

"Nothing, now that you've explained it."

"Another thing—I know Farini has his stooges. Let me tell you, mister, that Cyrus has his own rough boys. I saw a couple of them at his stone hideaway when Joan and I would visit. I never learned their names. Stock manipulations were the least of that bastard's crimes."

"My thought exactly," I lied. "I think Vogel and his buddies are heading up a dead-end trail."

"You would be doing me a favor by telling them that. They sure hate Farini, don't they?"

"So did Luther."

"I know. And I know why. But our noble guardians of the law were involved in that, too, weren't they?"

"That's what Luther claimed. Well, I won't hold you up any longer. Thanks for listening."

"Anytime," he said.

I would call him anytime I wanted more bull. What a liar! I should have taken a course on it from him. He could have earned my five grand.

As a connoisseur of the art, however, I felt that line — "I never learned their names" — was below his usual standard. If he could invent fictitious Allingham thugs, he should have been able to come up with believable fictitious names. They would have kept the trail just as blind. Despite Duane Detterwald's scorn, I considered myself rather clever at names.

I went back to the weights and my ruminations. I had to keep revising my scenarios. Most cases stay truer to form, the good guys in the white hats, the bad guys in the black hats. All the principals in this case wore black hats.

I had a hazy theory, but it might develop into another errant scenario. It would be wise to let it simmer for a while. I went out for a short jog, came home and swam ten lengths of the pool.

Half an hour later, while I was still searching out the soft spots in my new theory, Corey rang our doorbell. He looked worried.

"You've been fired," I guessed.

"No. But I didn't work today, and Max Kronen came to the house to lecture me."

"Come in," I said. "A lecture from Max should be interesting. We'll interpret it over a cup of coffee. Somehow, I have never thought of Max as a father figure."

Over coffee in our cool den, Corey said, "The way he explained it, Baker was tied up with Joe Farini. He said he, too, had been working for Farini, but his ethics wouldn't permit him to continue once he learned that Farini was involved in a criminal activity."

I smiled. "Did you ask him what the criminal activity was?"

Corey nodded. "But he explained that it would be unethical for him to reveal privileged information."

"Did you point out that it would be unethical for him to hide criminal activity that he was aware of from the police?"

"I didn't think of that. He did tell me he was thinking of taking it to the police."

"Not in this town, he wouldn't. They don't pay enough. And then, I suppose, he went on to lecture you?"

"Oh, yes. Heavy stuff! How a young man starting out in a profession with a long tradition had to be careful to establish a reputation for integrity if he hoped to build a solid clientele."

"Corey, I hope you didn't believe any of that bilge."

"A little. He was very persuasive."

"The man has switched sides! He was trying to get you off the case. I wonder how much Allingham paid him to switch?"

Corey stared at me. "That son of a bitch! Why didn't I think of that?"

"You're still in the learning stage. Did he tell you he was going back to Los Angeles?"

Corey nodded.

"Let's check him out," I said, and picked up the phone.

Information gave me the number and I dialed it. A woman's voice said, "Kronen Investigative Services."

"This is Bertrand Ehrlich," I told her. "Is Mr. Kronen available?"

"*Judge* Bertrand Ehrlich?" she asked.

"That's right. It's very important that I get in touch with Mr. Kronen today. Is he in the office?"

"He isn't, sir. He is out of town on a case."

"Damn it!" I said. "This is extremely important, and Max is the only person who can help me."

"I could have him phone you, sir."

"I won't be home. I'm not home now. Isn't there *any* way I can get in touch with him today?"

"He'll be at the Dunes Motel in Donegal Bay tonight. He might be there by now. You could try there." She gave me the phone number.

I thanked her and hung up. I told Corey what she had told me and added, "You tell Baker about Max's lecture. Don't tell him what we learned. I have another call to make."

"Okay. I don't want to go up against Max, Brock."

"I do."

He left for Baker's house. I phoned Duane Detterwald's office number. No answer. I got him at home. I told him, "That private investigator, Max Kronen, is back in your town. He's driving a gray Volvo with a San Fernando dealer's license frame. He'll be staying at the Dunes Motel tonight. If your friend Mike is up to any shenanigans, you had better alert him. Kronen is working for Cyrus Allingham now."

"What has Allingham got against Mike?"

"It's complicated," I said. "I'm not too clear on it, myself. But I suspect he's trying to get something on Alan Baker by tying Mike up with Felicia."

"I'll say that's complicated. Are you sober?"

"Trust me, Duane," I said. "You are my only fan in Donegal Bay."

"Okay," he promised. "I'll run right down there and talk with Mike."

Jan came home with that greedy look in her eyes again. "Guess who called me this morning and wants me to redecorate her house?"

"Princess Diana? Brooke Shields? Nancy Reagan?"

"Daphne Detterwald."

"Great!" I said. "I'm going up to Donegal Bay tonight to talk with Duane. We can go together and save on gas."

"I'll phone her to see if it's all right," she said.

It was. We had an early dinner and took Jan's car. The Mercedes, she explained patiently to me, would be more reassuring to a client willing to pay Kay Décor prices.

It was still light when we arrived at the Detterwalds' house, three houses north of Marilyn's unsold Colonial. Duane explained to Daphne that he was taking me down to show me some investment property on the beach.

"I talked with Mike," he told me, as we went down the steep, winding road. "I got nowhere. Jesus, that dago is dumb!"

"It might be time," I suggested, "to review old loyalties."

"That could be," he admitted. "We're a long way from high school. We got along well when Mike was Mr. Big. But after Duke Ellis put a stop to his career and I started to make a few bucks, I began to get the feeling that Mike resented me."

"Maybe he found out that you were the man who warned Felicia not to put the restaurant in his name."

"No. Only Felicia and I knew that, and she wouldn't tell him. Mike just has to be top dog."

We checked the cars in the restaurant parking lot and found no Volvo. We went to the Dunes Motel and the manager told us Max Kronen was occupying unit number twelve.

We could hear angry voices inside when I knocked on the door.

There was pleading in Max's voice when he called, "Come in. The door isn't locked."

I opened the door. Mike and Max were standing at the far end of the room, near the sliding glass door that led to the beach. Max was holding his stomach and there was blood slowly seeping from his nose.

"You damned fool!" Duane said to Mike. "Don't you know that a boxer's fists are considered lethal weapons in this state?"

"Shut up, Weasel," Mike said. "Who's your fat friend?" He paused to study me. "You? The guy who used to spar with Charlie Davis?"

"One and the same," I admitted. "Duane is right, Mike. You had better cool it. You could be in serious trouble."

"Get out of here," he said, "Both of you."

I shook my head.

Mike smiled, and sized me up, head to toes. "How many times have you been kayoed, big boy?"

"Several times," I said. "But never by a middleweight. I didn't come here to fight you. I came to talk with Max."

"Close the door on your way out," he said. "Your turn will come."

I shook my head again.

"You've got exactly five seconds. Go!"

"I'm not leaving, Mike," I told him. "Do you want to go outside and settle this?"

He smiled again, the happy warrior. "Oh, do I ever! Let's go."

I almost knew what his first punch would be when we stood there on the macadam of the parking lot. It would be the big overhand right. That could be the main reason Mike never got to the crown; he led too often with that club fighter's major weapon.

Duke Ellis had kept moving inside of it, bringing his hook along, slamming it into Mike's belly. That fight had been fought under the Marquis of Queensberry Rules, originated long ago by the Eighth Marquis of Queensberry.

To me, that particular marquis was famous only as the creep who had tried to destroy Oscar Wilde. His rules had no validity for me, and I didn't have a trained boxer's hook.

I did have a hard head. I moved inside Mike's opening haymaker and cracked several of his front teeth with the top of my head. He looked startled, and one hand went up to cover his mouth.

I stepped on his foot, to keep him from moving back, and put all I had into a right hand deep into his out-of-shape stomach. He went to his knees slowly, holding his stomach with both hands, flecks of blood from his torn lips splattering out as he exhaled. Then he fell forward on his face.

Duane stood there, staring down almost pityingly at his fallen hero. He said softly, "You know something? Tonight's the first time that Mike ever called me Weasel."

Chapter Thirteen

MAX was standing in his open doorway when we got back, holding a washcloth wrapped around ice cubes to his bleeding nose.

"I never thought I'd be glad to see you, Callahan," he told me. "That bastard might have killed me. He's crazy! I wonder who put him wise to me?"

"I did," Duane said. "He's a friend of mine—or was. What kind of trouble is he in now?"

"None I've discovered so far," Max said. "Or at least none I can prove. And that's all I will tell you about that." He looked at me. "Why are you here?"

"Because I warned you to lay off Corey Raleigh—and you didn't."

"I didn't lay a finger on him!"

"You conned him, Max."

He shrugged. "All right! I conned him. Look who's talking! You think I don't know your reputation? You conned plenty of people."

"Not anybody in my line of work, not if it would cost him his job. And never a kid. Did Corey scare you? Is that why you tried to talk him into quitting?"

"Don't be silly."

"And you switched sides," I went on. "I know your reputation, too, Max. You sold out to the highest bidder again."

"Prove it," he said. "Sue me."

"You stay clear of Corey. I don't want him to turn into another you."

"Okay." He sneered. "Let him sweat it out in his garage office, taking advice from you. I got four people working for me."

"All four working at minimum, I'll bet. Lock your door, Max. Anthony might be planning a comeback."

As we climbed into his 280-Z, Duane said, "You came up here and learned nothing."

"I hadn't actually planned to come up," I explained. "But when Jan told me about Daphne's interest, I suggested we come up together. Remember, this is a community-property state. Jan will make the trip worthwhile for me."

He shook his head. "Not Jan. She wouldn't overcharge me."

His crystal ball was unclouded. On the way home, Jan said, "I love that couple. I am going to refurnish that place at our cost. This will be the very first time I have ever done that."

Duane and Jan had shared their historic firsts on the same summer evening. I said nothing.

"Why," she asked, "did Duane lie to Daphne? You two didn't go down to the beach to look at any property."

"I suppose he was trying to shelter her from knowledge of the cruel outside world."

"His beauty in the buff? She's been there before."

"Duane is sentimental," I explained. "Look how long he has stuck with Mike. How did that dopey Mike get to be elected president of your senior class?"

"Duane ran his campaign. What kind of trouble is Mike in now?"

"I don't know. I hope it's more than he can handle."

Loyalties, loyalties.... I remembered when I was sixteen and my best friend of eight years had proved to be less than a friend. Why, I asked my mother, had my friend changed?

She had explained it to me, and the years since had proved her right. People don't change. It is only that it takes longer to find out about some of them.

The night was bright, the moon was full. Several outdoor parties were visible in the spreads that bordered Ranch Road.

Duane had rescued Daphne from the real world and brought her to this bucolic playland retreat. It was possible that he had not done her a favor.

Alan had made an honest woman out of Felicia. Honest was the wrong word; he had made a legal woman out of Felicia. Perhaps she had decided that illegality was more fun. It seemed clear now that Mike had decided it was.

Unless he deals in gullible, senile widows, it is hard to hate a con man. They rarely resort to violence, and their victims are usually as larcenous (but not as clever) as the perpetrators. Bilking a bigot like Cyrus Reed Allingham out of a portion of his excessive wealth was almost a form of public service.

But not blackmail. And certainly not blackmail that may have caused the death of an innocent. But had he been? Had Luther Barnum really been an innocent?

I should have spent more time this morning in Rubio's Rendezvous. Maybe Luther had played a major part in the supporting cast of his own tragedy. He could have been a principal.

"Why so quiet?" Jan asked. "What are you thinking about?"

"About murder," I said.

"I don't want to hear any more. Go back to your thinking."

I had no thoughts left that would make things clearer. Tomorrow, I would ask Corey if Baker had revealed anything new. And I would go back to Rubio's. To quote Marilyn's idol, I would think about it tomorrow.

Despite the full moon, which usually keeps me awake, I slept soundly through the night, thanks to my afternoon workouts and my two-punch bout in Donegal Bay.

I phoned Corey before breakfast and asked him about his visit with Alan Baker.

"I didn't get in to see him," he told me. "Mrs. Baker's car was on the driveway and I didn't want to blow my cover. He'll call me when the coast is clear. He always does." He paused. "I have a hunch."

"Let's hear it. Hunches are my specialty."

"I think you and I are working on separate cases. I think Mr.

Baker is crazy jealous, and I don't blame him. If I had a wife as pretty as she is, I'd keep her in a vault."

"Your instincts are almost as sharp as mine," I said, "but the cases could be connected." I told him about my confrontation with Anthony on the parking lot and added, "Keep in touch."

"Natch," he said. "Until I can build up my weight, you're a handy man to have around."

Jan seemed preoccupied at the breakfast table. "Is something troubling you?" I asked.

"Audrey. I'm not sure she'll go along with my no-markup deal for the Detterwalds."

"You could threaten to quit if she didn't."

"Don't be absurd. Audrey is much more than a boss to me. She is my friend!"

"Then compromise. Does Audrey charge her friends the same markup that she charges strangers?"

"I don't know," Jan said thoughtfully. "But thanks for the ploy. I'm going to ask her."

She left for work. I drank coffee and read the *Times*.

The Dodgers had won last night, the Angels had lost. In two weeks the Rams would be heading for training camp, preparing for battles that might carry them to another Super Bowl. I had never played in a Super Bowl. To compensate for that, neither had I been forced to play two games in one week. The networks had not *owned* the game in those days; they had been minor participants.

The Russians were growling again, sending the price of gold up, the value of the dollar down. Manufacturers of home security systems were doing a land office business. Two of the oldest and most respected newspapers in the nation were going out of business. Hollywood's alleged elite were now paying two thousand dollars an ounce for the cocaine they sniffed at their fancy parties.

That was enough of that; it was time to head for the orderly world of Rubio's Rendezvous.

The Judge was on his bench at the end of the bar, reading the book section of the *New York Times* and drinking coffee.

Rubio was standing at the near end, reading the *Racing Form*. Four elderly regulars were playing pinochle at the round table farthest from the door.

"Welcome," Rubio greeted me. "Anything new?"

I shook my head. "Nothing that points a finger. I talked with Maria Lopez."

He nodded sadly. "I know. She told me you did. The language that woman uses!"

"Did she tell you about the bulge under the man's field jacket?"

"No." He stared at me. "Bulge?"

"Bulge. Maybe a bottle of cognac. I'd have a cup of coffee, but I've already had three cups."

"I have instant cocoa. It's not bad."

"Fine." I took the stool next to The Judge, Rubio set the cocoa in front of me. It wasn't bad—if compared with Mike's clam chowder.

The Judge folded his paper neatly and laid it on the bar. "I've been thinking back," he said. "We don't have a *reason*, do we? We don't have a motive."

"Only a connection," I said. "The Allinghams."

He nodded agreement. "Lucy wrote to Luther almost every week. She sent him money. But she didn't come down here when he died."

"There was no funeral," I explained. "Not even a memorial service."

"We are planning a memorial service," he said. "But if you were Luther's only living relative, wouldn't you have come down?"

"I guess."

"Women are different," Rubio the male chauvinist said.

"Not much different," The Judge said. "Though I will grant you they are less emotional than men."

"*Less?*" Rubio said.

"Less," The Judge decreed. "Do women cry at football games? Do they scream?"

"Some do," Rubio argued. "The pom-pom girls do."

The Judge frowned. "That's enough of that. Let us proceed. Lucy tells Luther in a letter that her employer is being black-mailed. Why?"

"My theory," I offered, "is that Cyrus Allingham has been guilty of some serious violation of the law that has never been uncovered. Alan Baker must have known about it."

"You were thinking of some financial shenanigans?"

"Probably."

"Think of it this way. If it was something financial, it would be a weak threat. Think of the high-priced attorneys he can afford, the creative accountants he can summon."

"True."

"We won't discard it," he decided. "We'll hold it in abeyance. I have been considering another line of inquiry. About a week ago, a reporter came to see Luther at the hotel."

"A local reporter?" I asked.

"No. He was working for one of those scandal magazines, one of those foul weeklies that are displayed on racks next to the checkout counters at supermarkets."

"Which women buy by the millions," Rubio said.

The Judge glared at him.

"Did you learn the man's name?" I asked. "Do you know what magazine he worked for?"

He shook his head. "Luther was unusually secretive about that part. Which makes it a valid line of inquiry to me. It would take more work, more research than those shoddy sheets give to their stories to untangle the complicated financial manipulations of a Cyrus Allingham. It has to be something else."

"Something important enough for Allingham to have Luther murdered?"

"We were discussing the 'why,' not the 'who,'" he pointed out.

"Farini is still my favorite for the who," Rubio said.

"Farini," The Judge said, "is always your favorite for every bad thing that happens in this town." He turned to me. "I questioned the desk clerk at the hotel and two residents who were in the lobby when Luther talked with the reporter. Nothing. No usable description, no name, *nothing*."

"Nothing," Rubio repeated. "Which means we are nowhere."

The Judge sighed. "You and your quick and easy solutions. We are closer than we were."

Chapter Fourteen

I stopped in at the station, but Bernie was out of his office. I was walking across the station parking lot to my car when this gleaming new Rolls Royce, still carrying the dealer's temporary plate, pulled into the space next to mine.

It was Joe Farini. He looked at me without interest when he stepped from his car, two hundred and fifty pounds of expensive attorney disdain.

"Classy wheels!" I told him. "You have proved it, Joe. Crime does pay."

"Some people inherit," he said coolly. "Some people have to earn their own way. I would suggest you save your scorn for the inheritance parasites."

"Your point, fairly scored," I admitted. "Is it true that the San Fernando flash has deserted you?"

"If you are speaking of Mr. Kronen, shamus, he had to go back to be with his sick wife. She is in a Los Angeles hospital."

I smiled. "He conned you, Joe. He switched sides. Max doesn't have a wife." I climbed into my car.

"Brock, wait a minute—" he called.

I waved at him and drove off the lot. Keep your opponent off balance; I had learned that in my first year of high-school football.

Had Max switched sides before we had discovered it? He had been up in Donegal Bay, checking on Mike, before that. He could have learned from Farini that Allingham's counterthreat involved Mike and then gone to Donegal Bay to confirm it, or even to alert Mike.

Now that he was working the other side of the street, he

would be working to get confirmation for Allingham. Allingham must have been armed with nothing but a rumor. A rumor is not enough ammunition against a client of Joe Farini. Joe would have the heavy ammunition — the facts — before he sat down at the bargaining table.

Max had told us last night that he'd discovered nothing about Mike he could prove. It could have been a lie, but the truth seemed more likely. He was staying there overnight, still on the case. For all I knew, of course, he could be planning a triple-cross by inviting himself into Mike's scam.

Cyrus Allingham had assured me that if he needed my help he would call on me. His daughter had told me that she would phone when Lucy was ready to be questioned. But neither of them had given me their unlisted telephone number. What they had told me, in effect, was "Don't call me; I'll call you."

I had a greedy acquaintance at the telephone company who'd supplied me with unlisted numbers before. I phoned the company and asked for him. He was, a brusque voice at the other end of the line informed me, no longer with the company. I didn't ask why.

I told Mrs. Casey I wouldn't be home for lunch and headed for Veronica Village. Lucy Barnum could be the key to this case.

In the stone outpost that served as a telephone booth, I was informed by Joan that neither her father nor Lucy was at home, but she would like to talk with me.

In the high-ceilinged living room, she opened with a question: "What is going on, Mr. Callahan?"

"Could you be more specific?" I said.

"This man, this Mr. Kronen. First he comes up here as a representative for that lawyer, Farini, and now I have reason to believe he is working for my father."

"Max Kronen," I told her, "is an investigator who almost lost his license three years ago. He has a reputation in the profession as a man who puts his own self-interest above loyalty to a client. With Max, self-interest translates into money."

"Oh, yes!" she said. "Self-interest, that's the dominant theory today. And my father, who spends thousands and thousands of dollars trying to instill some of our fundamental values back into this sick society—he is maligned as some kind of tyrant."

"Not by everybody," I soothed her, "not by a long shot. There aren't that many Alan Bakers in the world."

"Do you have any idea," she asked, "what Alan has learned that he thinks might damage my father's reputation?"

I shook my head. "Possibly some complicated financial deal. Hasn't he told you *anything* about it?"

"Nothing," she said. "But I suppose the newspapers will have a field day with it, no matter how little substance it has. You don't think it has anything to do with Lucy's uncle, do you?"

"That's what I came up to find out. Will Lucy be home sometime today?"

"Not for two weeks," she told me. "Father thought she needed some relief from the turmoil of the last few days. So he treated her to a long-overdue vacation, two weeks in Hawaii."

"Would it be possible for me to phone her at her hotel there?"

"I doubt it. Father thinks she should not be disturbed. The poor girl was close to hysteria when she left. But he'll be home sometime tomorrow. If he feels it won't distress Lucy, I'll have him phone you."

Don't call me; I'll call you. I didn't ask for their phone number. I stood up and told her, "I have to leave. I'm due in Donegal Bay in twenty minutes."

There was a sudden interest in her eyes and in her voice. "Donegal Bay? Father planned to build there before he found this property. Do you have friends there?"

"One friend," I said, "a former boxer named Mike Anthony. It's possible your father knows him, if he is also a boxing fan. Thanks for talking with me. I hope it hasn't been too much of an intrusion."

"Not in this house. You will always be welcome here, Mr. Callahan. As I told you on your last visit, my father will be so sorry that he missed you."

And so surprised, I thought, *when you tell him Mike Anthony is a friend of mine.* That ought to keep him off balance, and me off his mailing lists.

I hadn't planned to stop at Donegal Bay on the way home. But with Lucy Barnum in Hawaii, the search for Luther's killer was temporarily at a halt. And the day was young.

It was warm and sunny at the freeway end of Ranch Road. The mist began to drift in from the ocean and the temperature to drop at the crest of the first rise. It grew cooler, and the fog became thicker on the long climb to the bluff. Driving down that narrow, steep, curving road to the beach would be hazardous today.

Forge on, self-anointed knight in tarnished armor.... I switched on the fog lights, put the car into low gear, and kept my foot on the brake pedal. I kept the speed constant at five miles an hour.

The door to Duane's office was not locked, but he wasn't there. Through the thin wall that separated it from the bait store, I heard the sound of angry voices. One of them was Duane's.

I went out to the covered porch that served both places and through the open door of the store.

Duane was standing in front of the counter, facing an obviously discomfitted nephew. At the far end of the counter, Laura was stacking reels in a glass display case, probably to steer clear of the argument.

Jeff looked up and saw me, and there was relief on his face. "Good morning, Mr. Callahan," he said. "You just walked in on a family feud."

Duane turned around. "Hi," he said. "Trouble?"

I shook my head. "Should I wait outside? I don't want to interrupt your discussion."

"You're not. I've said all I have to say—for the moment. Let's go to my office."

In his office, I said, "I could hear you through the wall. It sounded to me as though you were playing the heavy uncle."

"Kids!" he said. "You know what those two did? They hit Felicia for fifty thousand dollars! And I'll give you track odds that that damned Mike is mixed up in it."

"Fifty thousand? For what?"

"For a boat, a charter fishing boat. I don't know what they cost. A friend of mine told me he's sure that Mike put some money in it, too."

"Alan Baker let Felicia do that?"

"He's got nothing to say about it. Felicia's money is her own. She had two short-term rich husbands before Alan. That dopey Felicia never said one word about it to me. How can those kids hope to pay her back with charter-boat rentals?"

"Maybe it isn't a loan. Maybe she'll be a partner and share in the profits."

"She couldn't live long enough to get that kind of money back. What burns me is that those kids would sucker a friend of mine into that kind of deal. And I learn about it *after* the fact. They probably explained to her that I wouldn't stand still for a deal that risky."

"Are you going to question Mike about it?"

"We're not talking to each other," he said. "Not anymore. I've overlooked a lot of his shortcomings over the years. This time he went too far."

He sat in his chair behind the desk. "Damn it, my doctor told me my heart couldn't take much agitation. Sit down, Brock, and I'll try to relax."

I sat in his customer's chair. I said soothingly, "It's Felicia's money. Let her worry about it."

"I know," he admitted wearily. "But she is my friend and they took advantage of that. Wouldn't that burn you?"

"It would."

"What are you doing in town?" he asked.

"I decided to stop here on my way home from Veronica Village." I told him about my visit to the castle and what I had learned there. "Lucy," I explained, "was my last best hope on the Barnum murder. I sure as hell can't phone every hotel in the islands to find out if she's registered."

"I have friends on Oahu who could," he told me, "*real* friends. They run a chain of hotels over there and can phone the others. I'll find out for you and let you know." He rubbed the back of his neck. "I'm going home for lunch. Why don't you eat with us?"

"Not today, thanks. But let me follow your taillights up the road. It scared me plenty, coming down."

"Me, too," he admitted. "I hope Mike tries it—and goes over the edge."

"We'll let Cyrus Allingham take care of Mike," I said. "Horses for courses, Duane. Dirty men for dirty jobs."

"Right," he agreed. "You stick with that end of this mess. I'll keep an eye on this end. I'll phone my friends in Hawaii today and report to you as soon as I learn anything."

I followed the glowing taillights of the Datsun up the shrouded road and came out to clearer air at the top. I waved good-bye to Duane and headed for home.

Fifty thousand dollars for a boat? I had no idea what a charter fishing boat would cost, but that seemed high. The only time I had priced boats, they had cost about a thousand dollars a lineal foot.

I knew even less about how much income a charter boat could clear in a day. That would depend, of course, on how many anglers it could hold, how many signed up, and how much each was charged for the trip.

Mike was a wanderer, fretting to leave his isolated home. It didn't seem likely to me that he would stay around long enough to help pay off a fifty-thousand-dollar loan. Most of the people in this area had their own boats, for fishing and pleasure.

I was back on the freeway when I saw a car that looked like Corey's heading the other way. I recognized him when he came abreast on the other side of the divider. My first thought was that he was following Felicia again. But the only vehicles within his range of vision were two campers, a truck, and four cars too old and cheap to be carrying Mrs. Alan Baker.

If he was heading for Donegal Bay, it was possible that Alan Baker may have learned about Felicia's extravagance and sent Corey up to check it out.

I didn't want Corey to go up against Mike Anthony; the urge to follow him was strong. But the next exit was two miles down the road. And, as Corey had told me, he was a big boy now.

Chapter Fifteen

MRS. Casey insisted on being told whenever I wasn't planning to come home for lunch, and resented my coming when I wasn't expected. I stopped at Hannah's Hamburger Heaven for a cheeseburger and a milkshake.

One bite of the cheeseburger was all I could handle. My stomach was growling, my ulcer burning. I drank the shake slowly. Frustration gnawed at me. All of that mileage behind me and what had I accomplished?

Allingham had his double-walled fortress — one wall of stone, one of money. And why should it matter to me who won this blackmail showdown? They were both enemy camps to me. The innocents, if any, in this mélange of characters were the late Luther Barnum and his cousin. One was dead, the other out of reach.

What about Felicia Baker? "Innocent" might be a misuse of the word, applied to her. But judging by her charity to Mike and now to Duane's nephew, neither could she be considered larcenous.

From the wall phone at Hannah's, I phoned the Baker house and she answered. So Corey couldn't have been following her. I asked, "Would it be possible for me to speak with you alone?"

"Why alone? Is it something about Alan?"

"It might be something you don't want him to know about. I've just come from a visit with Duane and he is really steaming. He learned about the money you loaned his nephew."

"That's none of his damned business," she told me. "It's my

money and I love those kids. Duane is a good friend of mine, but he's turning into a miser. I liked him better when he was a horse player."

"Okay," I said. "I just thought I'd let you know."

"Wait," she said. "There's more, isn't there? There are things bothering you besides that, aren't there?"

"There are. But they involve Alan, and I'm sure you know him a lot better than I do."

"Not as well as I should, the way it's beginning to look. And I didn't tell him about the money I loaned Jeff and Laura. Could we meet somewhere?"

"We could meet at my house," I suggested. "We'll be chaperoned. The housekeeper will be there."

She laughed. "Couldn't you send her to the store or something?"

"I could try," I promised, "but she's a stubborn woman." I gave her the address.

She was closer to our house than I was. She was waiting in front of it in a yellow Citroën when I pulled into the driveway. She walked across the lawn and met me at the front door.

She was smiling, her green eyes glinting impishly. "I rang your bell. Nobody answered. How much time do we have?"

"I am a faithful husband," I said sadly, "and this is the first time I've ever had reason to regret it."

She sighed. "It's not a total loss. I will see the inside of a Jan Bonnet house. Daphne told me Jan is redoing hers."

Mrs. Casey was coming across the lawn from our neighbor's house. "I'm sorry, Mr. Callahan," she said, "but I didn't know you would be home for lunch."

"I've had lunch," I told her. "This is Mrs. Baker. Perhaps she'd like some coffee."

"I would, thank you," Felicia said.

Mrs. Casey smiled. "Meaning no impertinence, Mrs. Baker, but you're Irish, aren't you?"

"Mostly," Felicia said. "How could you tell?"

"Only the Irish are that beautiful," Mrs. Casey explained. "I'll go make your coffee now."

She went to the kitchen. We went into the living room. Felicia stood there, admiring it.

"I'd take you through the rest of the rooms," I said, "but that would include the bedrooms and Mrs. Casey is a little prudish. Let's sit out in back. It's cooler there."

We sat in the shade near the house. I said, "One of the things that's troubling me is Alan getting involved with Joe Farini. He has a very unsavory reputation."

"Involved?" She frowned. "I've met Mr. Farini only once, that afternoon you came to the house. That day, all he and Alan talked about was another threat that Cyrus Allingham was making. Ever since Alan divorced Joan, that has been going on. That old monster won't give up. He still resents the divorce settlement he gave Alan. What do you mean by 'involved'?"

"I could have been misinformed," I said. "Did you know that Joe Farini hired a detective? That detective is now working for Allingham, checking on Mike Anthony."

"That's too complicated for me. Do you mean that this detective is working for both of them?"

"No. He changed sides. He switched over to the big money. Did Duane tell you about the fight I had with Mike up at Donegal Bay?"

She stared at me. "Nobody told me. What's going on? Why are they keeping all this from me? Do they think I'm the village virgin? I've been around, and in some pretty rough places, too."

"You've certainly weathered it well," I told her. "The way it happened, Duane and I were trying to talk Mike out of beating up the detective. Mike got lippy and I had to put him to sleep. He's in some kind of trouble up there which I'm sure Allingham thinks he can use as ammunition against your husband."

"But Alan doesn't even know Mike! It doesn't make sense."

"You know Mike," I pointed out. "You could be Allingham's target."

"I *knew* Mike," she corrected me. "I haven't talked to him in two years. Even when I visit the Detterwalds, I make sure that Mike won't be there before I go up."

"That afternoon at your house," I reminded her, "you told

me that you didn't know what he was doing now. You lied."

"I had to, in front of Alan. Duane talks so much about the old days that Alan has this absurd notion that Mike was the great love of my life. The truth of the matter is that he doesn't even rank in the top ten."

Mrs. Casey brought our coffee, gazed at Felicia for a few seconds, sighed, and went back to the kitchen.

"Duane doesn't like Alan much, does he?" I asked.

She shook her head. "He never drops in when he's in town anymore. But he still likes Mike. I'll take Alan over Mike any day."

I smiled. "Or night? Is Alan in the top ten?"

"Don't get vulgar, Callahan. I bought Mike that restaurant three years ago. Strictly for auld lang syne. Duane insisted I keep the title in my name. I'm glad he did, now. Is that the connection Allingham thinks he has? I had a hunch Mike was in trouble. Is it serious?"

"Maybe not yet. But Duane and I think he's heading for it. The rumor up in Donegal Bay is that Mike is going to be a partner in that charter-boat venture you financed."

"So what? Is that illegal? None of this makes sense."

"To me, either," I admitted. "But it might be wise if you alerted Laura and Jeff about Mike's... propensity for getting into trouble."

She said, "I'm sure that won't be necessary. If skinflint Duane knows about it, he has probably read them the riot act."

"You are demeaning a great little guy," I told her.

"I know. But he's so stuffy these days! We used to have so much fun when Mike was a contender and Duane a horse player—"

And you a hustler, I thought. *Those golden days!*

"What are you smirking about?" she asked.

"I'm remembering my own youth."

"I'll bet you are!" She stood up. "I have to go. Alan will be

home soon and I want to get my questions ready for that sneak.
Once a con man, always a con man. Right, Callahan?"

I smiled again.

"You bastard!" she said. "Alan was right about you. You are
one sarcastic bastard—even when you don't open your
mouth."

"I know. But you like me, don't you?"

"I do."

"It's mutual," I told her.

I went to the door with her and came back to finish my coffee.
Mrs. Casey came to pick up Felicia's cup but mainly to say, "A
real Irish beauty, isn't she?"

"That she is. And tricky, too, like all the Irish."

"Speak for yourself," she said. "Not for the rest of us."

"Why don't you pour us a couple of slugs of that good Irish
whiskey you keep in the kitchen," I suggested, "and we'll discuss
it. Unless, of course, you think it would be tricky if we don't
tell Jan."

"There is necessary tricky and unnecessary tricky," she informed me loftily. "I'll be right back."

We sat in the shade and discussed the novelty of a Polish
pope. We talked about how the Protestants and agnostics in
this mixed neighborhood were finally sending their kids to
Catholic schools, where the disciplinary problems of our time
were solved in the old-fashioned way—learn or burn!

Then she went to her room to watch the late-afternoon fea-
ture movie on the tube, starring Spencer Tracy.

I sat and tried to fit the pieces of information I had garnered
today into some semblance of a pattern.

There were too many ill-fitting pieces in this puzzle that
couldn't be matched up. I hoped I had stirred up some new
allegiances today that would separate the white hats from the
black. Too many of them were still gray.

Felicia now knew that Alan was up to no good. Farini knew
that Kronen had gone over to Allingham. And Allingham

would wonder about my supposed friendship with Mike Anthony.

Felicia had told me that she had a hunch Mike was in trouble. If she hadn't seen him in two years, what were the grounds for her hunch?

I suspected that Alan had confided in her at least enough to give her an inkling of what was going on. A tricky lass, that Felicia. But maybe it was Mrs. Casey's necessary tricky. I wanted to think so.

I was dozing on the couch when Jan came home. "Mrs. Casey told me you had a visitor this afternoon," she opened.

I sat up and yawned and stretched. I knew what was coming. I said, "Mrs. Casey told you the truth."

"The most beautiful woman she has seen in years is the way she described her. Felicia Baker? I don't remember her as *that* beautiful."

"She isn't," I said. "And I don't like the way she does her hair."

She studied me suspiciously. "You mean like mine?"

"Of course not! I mean the way you used to wear it. Your new way is much more flattering."

She sniffed. "You're sure full of it today, aren't you? Why did she come to see you?"

"Because I suggested it. I'm trying to round up all the allies I can find in this stupid, ugly war. Let's not quibble. Did Audrey agree to a lower markup on the Detterwald deal?"

"She did. We will make only a modest profit."

I didn't ask her what Kay Décor considered modest. The word no longer had meaning in the inflated eighties.

Duane phoned after dinner. "That kid you were talking about when you first came up here, that gangly kid driving a gray Plymouth—does his car have a broken taillight lens?"

"It does. Is he up there now?"

"Yup. I saw him checking in at the Dunes Motel when I was coming home for dinner. Kronen's car is parked there, too.

Kronen I can understand. But why the kid? Maybe Felicia is up here seeing Mike."

"Felicia is home," I told him. "I talked with her this afternoon. She explained that she didn't tell you about the fifty thousand dollars because she thinks that you are getting too conservative in your dotage."

"Don't believe everything that Felicia tells you. And next time you see her, remind her that I *earned* my money."

"She earned some of hers, too, Duane," I reminded him.

"But how? If she had my looks, she would have been servicing winos. I heard from Hawaii. If Lucy Barnum is staying in a hotel there, it must be a flea bag. No hotel with running water has her registered."

"Thanks," I said. "I might be up there tomorrow. My protégé is still kind of green."

Chapter Sixteen

"As long as you're going up there," Jan said at breakfast, "would you come down to the shop first and pick up some samples for Daphne? And tell her I'll be up as soon as I finish the house I'm working on now. It shouldn't take longer than two more days."

"Yes, ma'am," I said.

"And tell her that delphinium blue we talked about will never go with that Oriental rug she wants to keep, because—"

"No!" I interrupted. "I will give her the message about two days and deliver the samples. The rest you can tell her over the phone. You can dial direct and deduct the expense from your modest markup. Operater-assisted calls cost more."

"Okay, master!"

Master? My rear seat and deck were crammed with samples when I headed for Donegal Bay. Carpet samples, drapery samples, furniture upholstery samples, tile and oak and vinyl floor samples. Master? Modest? Old Noah Webster must be turning in his grave.

Lucy Barnum was not staying at a major hotel in Hawaii. That didn't mean she wasn't there. Our fiftieth state was a haven for many of Allingham's true believers and contributors to his cause.

But would they accept a maid as a houseguest?

Duane wasn't there when I arrived. Daphne helped me carry the samples into the house. I told her about Jan being busy for the next two days and added, "She also said something about a rug you have, an Oriental, that won't blend with the delphinium blue you must have discussed with her."

"Damn it!" she said. "Duane loves that rug. And he's already moaning about cost. He's getting so chintzy!"

"Tell him not to fret," I said. "I have it on good authority that you are going to get the lowest markup in Kay Décor history. It will be very modest."

"You tell him. He won't believe me. He thinks I am a *terrible* shopper."

Duane was talking with a customer in his office. I went into the store next-door. Laura was sitting in an old wicker rocking chair, reading a paperback novel.

She looked up and smiled. "Mr. Callahan! Did you come to buy or to rent or to talk?"

"To talk," I said. "Has the family feud cooled off?"

She shook her head. "Not yet. Jeff is so — so bull-headed! We're not getting rich here, but we're still eating. And this is what he always claimed he wanted." She made a face. "Men!"

"I know," I agreed. "We are terrible creatures. Is Mike Anthony going to be involved in your new enterprise?"

"I guess so. I don't like him. From what I heard about your meeting at the Dunes, I guess you don't, either."

"He's been a bad friend to Duane," I told her. "Duane has been Mike's guardian angel for years. Bad friends make bad partners."

"Tell that to my bull-headed roomie."

"I will right now, if he's around."

She shook her head. "He's over at the Rusty Anchor, talking with Mike and some man who came here and picked up Jeff half an hour ago. He was Mexican, I think. At least his car had Mexican plates on it. A Cadillac DeVille, no less!"

"Laura," I said, "Mike Anthony is being watched by a private detective working for Cyrus Allingham. You tell Jeff that. He could be heading for big trouble."

She stared at me. "Cyrus Allingham? That man who lives in the castle in Veronica Village? Why would he have Mike watched?"

"I don't know. I can only guess that he must have some information about what Mike was doing—or plans to do. It would be a bad time for you two to team up with Mike. Tell Jeff to back off for a while."

Duane appeared in the open doorway. "Laura, will you listen for my phone? I—"

Then he saw me. "Brock! I didn't expect you this early. I have to show a couple of houses. It shouldn't take more than an hour."

"I'll be here," I said.

When he left, I told Laura, "Duane and I are trying to find out the connection between Allingham and Mike. Please do your best to convince Jeff not to make any decision for a while."

"I'll try," she said. "But I think it's a lost cause."

Another ally, I hoped. That is, if they had what today's unmarried roommates call a 'meaningful relationship.' I walked out and walked down to one of the side streets to where I could get a view of the Rusty Anchor parking lot. The DeVille with the Mexican plates was there.

A quarter of a block down the street from the lot, I saw a car that looked like Corey's. I started across the parking lot toward it just as a man came out of the restaurant and walked toward the Cad.

I knew who he was. Mike had a picture of him behind his bar, being slammed through the ropes by Mike's overhand haymaker.

"Chico Maracho?" I asked.

The black eyes in his olive face studied me doubtfully, almost suspiciously. "Yes. And you?"

"Only a fan," I said. "I saw you fight Mike in San Diego. I'll bet you're here for a rematch."

The doubt left his face. He smiled. "No. We are both retired and friends now. Are you a fighter?"

"I was. For about eight months. I'm a friend of Mike's. My name is Greg Hudson. Are you still involved in boxing down in Tijuana?"

He shook his head. "I'm in land development now. Mike convinced me in San Diego that boxing was not my proper trade."

"Maybe," I said. "But I still think that was a lucky punch that Mike tagged you with."

He smiled again. "It was lucky for me. I'm doing much better now. Adios, amigo."

The big car purred off; I walked over to Corey's car. He stared up at me. "Now what? Why are you in town?"

"I thought you might need some muscle. Have you seen that man I just talked with before now?"

He nodded. "He stayed at the motel last night. I couldn't get his name. He must be a fighter, or was. Did you notice the scar tissue over his eyes?"

"He was a fighter," I said. "His name is Chico Maracho. Is this the first time he's been at Mike's place?"

"First time here. Mike came over to the motel last night to talk with him, though."

"Was there somebody with Mike when he came, a young fellow?"

"Nobody. Why?"

"I think Mike's picked up a couple of partners. You report that to Alan Baker. Aren't you following Felicia anymore?"

He shook his head. "Anthony is my new assignment. Tell me, guru, am I supposed to know what's going on — or just follow orders?"

"That would depend on how long you want to live."

"Hey, Brock! That's a joke, isn't it?"

"Mostly. How are you eating? Not at Mike's, are you?"

"When he's not there, I can go in. I brought a lot of stuff from home. I don't like this case. But it pays so well!"

Jeff was now leaving the Anchor and walking up the road toward his shop. I told Corey, "That's one of Mike's new partners. His name is Jeff Randolph. His girl friend's name is Laura Prescott. They run that fishing shop next to the real-estate office. Put that in your report to Baker. He'll think you're earning your keep. I'm going to try to talk both of them out of teaming up with Anthony, but don't tell Baker that."

130

"And that Maracho; how does he fit into the picture?"

"That's what I hope to find out. Is Kronen still in town?"

"I haven't seen him around his morning. But he stayed at the motel last night. Maybe he changed cars."

"Maybe. Well, I have to make a phone call. Hang in there."

"Right! Hey, Brock, we're partners again, huh?"

I nodded. "I am now on your payroll. I'll try to keep an honest record of my expenses."

I left him with that sobering thought and went back to Duane's office. I phoned Bernie from there. I asked him, "Do you have any cop friends in Tijuana?"

"A couple. Why?

"There's an ex-pug named Chico Maracho who used to run a boxing gym down there. He now claims to be in land development. I would like the true word on him."

"Why?"

"That's private. But it might help to put Farini in the soup."

"Are you home?"

"No." I gave him Duane's number.

Angry words came through the thin wall again between me and the store. Then Jeff went storming out. A minute later, I heard the sound of a dune buggy revving in the soprano range. I walked over to find Laura still sitting in the wicker rocker. But now she was crying, her face in her hands.

"He'll be back," I said.

She shook her head. She didn't look up.

"He'll be back," I repeated, "unless he's a damned fool."

She looked up. "He is. Do you know what he told me? We'll use the boat for charter fishing in the daytime. Mike will be using it nights. Not every night, but nights. He must think I'm stupid."

"Did you ask him what Mike was going to use it for at night?"

"I did. He told me that was none of our business. If a renter brings back a boat in good condition, he said, what he does with it is none of our business."

"I hope he doesn't try to sell that story to the narcotic cops.

131

Did you ask him about that man who picked him up in the Cadillac?"

She shook her head. "Will he be their source?"

"He could be. He lives in Tijuana. I'm having him checked out right now. Do you have the boat yet?"

"No. Jeff's still dickering. The man wants twenty-seven thousand dollars for it."

"Which leaves twenty-three thousand of extra money. How will Jeff explain that to Felicia?"

"He told her the rest was needed to repair the pier and make it longer, so the water would be deep enough for the boat. That was a lie. The water's deep enough now for where he plans to moor the boat. He tried to make me believe it wasn't. Why?"

"Because he doesn't want to lose you. Couldn't you appeal to his parents?"

"They're traveling in Europe. He never got along with them. Uncle Duane is closer to Jeff than they are. And now Jeff's not even speaking to him."

"Did Jeff take any money with him when he went to Mike's?"

"I don't know. Why?"

"Because sources like to be paid in advance when they deal with small operators. You keep the faith, Laura. Your Uncle Duane and I will handle Jeff, even if we have to tie him to a post."

I was in Duane's office, reading his copy of the *Wall Street Journal*, when he came back.

"Lookers," he said. "Looky-lous, we call 'em. They're all lookers today, but nobody can afford to buy since the interest rates went crazy. Where is it going to end?"

"According to this tip sheet I'm reading, no end is in sight." I gave him the story of my adventures during his absence.

He frowned. "Maracho. The last I read, he was running a crummy gym for club fighters down in Tijuana."

"Not anymore, according to him. He claims to be in land development now."

"Chico Maracho in land development? He's even dumber than Mike! Hey, wait, you're not thinking narcotics? Not Jeff. No way!"

"Let's hope not. I phoned a cop friend of mine in San Valdesto. I'm waiting for his return call. He has police friends in Tijuana and I asked him to get me a line on Maracho."

Duane said quietly, "Not Jeff. Dear God, not Jeff! Not if he knows what he is getting into." He picked up the needle-pointed letter opener from his desk. "If Mike gets that kid involved in narcotics, he'll wind up with this in his throat."

"Easy, Duane. Remember what your doctor told you."

He took a deep breath.

I said, "I have some trivial good news for you. Jan is cutting her profit to the bone on you."

"Of course," he said. "She's *Jan*. Felicia thinks I'm a tightwad and so does Daphne. I'm doing okay, but I'm no Rockefeller. And if this ticker of mine runs out, I don't want Daphne to have to go back to erotic dancing."

"Is your heart that bad?"

He shrugged. "Who knows? Doctors make everything sound serious. How else can they con you into believing they are earning their exorbitant fees?"

The phone rang. Duane picked it up, said "Hello" and then "Yes." He handed me the phone.

It was Vogel. "About this Chico Maracho, he's had two arrests for assault, no convictions. He had one arrest for statutory rape with no conviction. And one for possession of cocaine, three months in the can plus three months' probation."

"Thanks, Bernie."

"There's one more tidbit that might interest you," he added. "Max Kronen was down there a couple of days ago asking around about Maracho. Is that how he's tied up with Farini?"

"I think so," I lied. I knew Bernie wouldn't have any interest in Allingham.

"You keep me informed, Brock."

"Don't I always?" I said, and hung up.

Chapter Seventeen

I repeated the items on the rap sheet to Duane.

"Those could apply to a lot of pugs today," he said, "including the cocaine. But I'd better warn Jeff."

"Wait until you cool off," I suggested. "There's no rush. He hasn't bought the boat yet. Maybe you should talk with Mike about it."

He shook his head. "I've said my last word to him. I'll talk with Laura. She's got more brains than Jeff and Mike together. Are you going home now?"

"After I talk with Corey. Stay cool now. Remember what the doctor told you."

I was on the porch and about to turn toward Duane's parking lot at the back of the building when I saw a gray Volvo parked about a hundred feet down the road.

Had Max been watching us? I went down there. He looked embarrassed when I reached the car.

"How was your trip to Mexico?" I asked. "Have fun?"

He glared up at me. "Who told you about that?"

"Farini," I said. "He had you followed. You never should have dumped him. Once he learned that you didn't have a wife, he turned really mean."

"Who told him that?"

"I did."

"What is it with you?" he asked. "Do you get your kicks out of bugging me? Jesus, there has to be some kind of sickness in you. I'll bet you're one of them pathological liars. You lie even when you don't get paid for it."

"It's the chronic disease of our trade," I explained. "Good hunting, Max."

Corey was still sitting in his car when I pulled up on the other side of the street from him. He looked weary.

"This is the boring part," I told him, "this sitting and waiting. You should have brought something to read."

"I listen to the radio," he said. "Kronen's in town. I saw his car go past about half an hour ago."

"I know. I've just finished talking with him. Why don't you get that taillight fixed? It's a dead giveaway."

"They want too much for those lenses."

"What do you care? Put it on the expense account."

"I never thought of that! Are you going to stay in town tonight?"

"Nope. You don't need me. Kronen won't bother you anymore."

"That's not what's bothering me," he said. "I have this feeling that I'm in over my head."

"It's a feeling we share," I said. "Maybe we'll get lucky."

Driving home, I thought back to Max's complaint. He had a point; I had gone out of my way to bug him. I was sure he had cut more corners in the trade than I had. But with four employees on his payroll, he was forced to cut more corners. To maintain a reasonable standard of ethics in this sordid profession, office expenses must be cut to the minimum.

It was almost noon now and I hadn't had lunch. My stomach was stronger today; I consumed two cheeseburgers and a malt at Hannah's without distress.

And where now? Felicia might be able to talk some sense into Jeff. She was his benefactor. There was also the possibility that she was his partner. Duane was our best hope to save Jeff.

Lucy, Lucy, where was that missing link? She had sent money to Luther and corresponded with him, but had not come down to arrange his funeral. Perhaps that decision had not been hers.

If what Luther had known about Farini had caused his death, Lucy had been his informant. The knowledge she had must have implicated Allingham. Why else would he have sent her away? And as the judicial assemblage at Rubio's Rendezvous had decided, the motive for the untimely demise of Luther Barnum was not his secret knowledge of complicated financial shenanigans.

The biggest threat to a man so obsessed with his pseudo-Puritan morality would be an attack on his own morality. Where was Lucy?

I was driving up Reservoir Road, heading for home, when I realized that only one person in town might know about Lucy's background, and I was about to drive past his house. I turned in at the Baker driveway.

Alan answered the door and looked at me coldly. "If you came to see Felicia," he said, "she isn't home."

"Why would I come here to see Felicia? Make sense, man!"

"She told me about the tête-à-tête at your house. She told me about that lie you told her."

"What lie?"

"That I had hired that Kronen character to check out Mike Anthony."

I said calmly, "The lie was hers, not mine. I told her Farini had hired Kronen and that Kronen had switched to Allingham. I told Farini the same thing—and I am sure he told you." I smiled at him. "That's not why you're miffed. There was no hanky-panky, Alan. Our housekeeper was home."

He said stiffly, "The thought of hanky-panky never entered my mind."

"Like hell it didn't. I am a happily married man and I intend to stay that way. I came here for only one reason. I am trying to locate Lucy Barnum. I hoped you might be able to help me with that."

He looked suprised. "Did she quit her job?"

"No. She is supposed to be vacationing in Hawaii, but I have reason to believe that isn't true. My only interest in this stinking mess is to find out who killed Luther. I thought you might know of some friends or relatives she might have gone to."

He was quiet, possibly considering how much truth he could reveal without self-incrimination. Then: "Both her parents were killed in an automobile accident while she was still working for us. I don't know of any other relatives, except for Luther. Her parents lived in Florian. She had one friend she used to write to down there." He frowned. "What was her name? It was a weird one. I remember now; it was Delilah. I've forgotten her last name. She was a school librarian."

"Thanks," I said. "How is Corey working out?"

"Satisfactorily. I'll say this for him, he's got something more than muscle going for him."

"True," I admitted. "But it was cruel of you to say it. You don't realize how sensitive I am. Take care, Alan."

Delilah somebody. Florian was a settlement of about twelve hundred citizens in the Ojai Valley. How many school librarians could there be named Delilah in a one-school town?

It was less than an hour's drive from here, but school was out for the summer, and it might take some lengthy and discreet questioning to learn Delilah's last name and her address. The next day would serve as well. The morning would be cooler in the Ojai Valley.

Jan had to attend a Children's Home Society meeting that night. I spent the evening reviewing on paper all the things I had learned or suspected since Alan's initial phone call.

The adversaries were more distinct now, their animosities more evident. But the motive for the murder of Luther Barnum was still shrouded. There was always the off chance that it had no connection with the Allingham-Baker feud. Murder for a wide variety of reasons was not uncommon on lower Main Street.

A heavy fog rolled in that night; a hazy overcast lingered when I took off for Florian. The gloom of the overcast was a welcome change. The Ojai Valley has been setting new heat records this summer.

The town was only about three miles from the freeway exit.

The homes were small, but not tract houses. The original inhabitants had migrated from New England and were immune to the California mass merchandising disease.

I drove to the school first to learn if there were summer sessions. There weren't. From there, I drove to the only filling station in town.

I pulled up next to the full-service pumps and told the young attendant to fill the tank and check under the hood.

There was a soft-drink vending machine in front of the building. "Want a Coke?" I asked him.

He grinned at me. "If you're buying, I'm drinking."

I went to the machine. He put the automatic cut-off nozzle into the filler pipe and came to the front of the car to lift the hood.

"Jesus!" he said, staring at the engine.

I handed him his Coke. "Nice, huh?"

"Oh, yes! What god hath wrought this? Mullaney, Meyer, Spelke?"

"Mostly Spelke. Mullaney wired that capacitative-discharge ignition. The blower is a Meyer X-9."

He shook his head in wonder. "And I thought my Roney Chev was a hot number! Do you live around here, or just passing through?"

"Passing through," I told him. "I sell textbooks and I took over this area last week. I came to see your school librarian. I didn't realize you don't hold summer sessions here."

"It's too hot," he explained. "You hit a lucky day. But Miss Kent lives in town. She's one of our customers. Couldn't you talk with her at her house?"

"Delilah Kent?" I asked him.

He nodded. "We have her address in the office. I'll get it for you."

The address he gave me was that of a small frame house in a section of small frame houses on Hampshire Street. There was no California stucco in sight.

A fleshy, middle-aged woman in tight shorts and a bulging halter was watering her gray lawn next-door as I went up the walk.

"Miss Kent isn't home," she called to me, "if that's who you came to see."

"Will she be back soon?" I asked. "I work for the Noel Publishing Company and we have a new fall list that I am sure would interest her. We've added some fiction this year."

"She didn't say exactly when she'd be back," the woman said. "One of her former high-school friends came down from Veronica Village and the two of them went off on a camping trip together."

"Thank you," I said.

I was walking back to my car when she called, "Wait! I just remembered. There's a school-board budget meeting Friday night and she told me last week she would have to attend that."

"Thank you again," I said. "I'll phone her on Friday to check before I come back. You've been having some miserable weather, haven't you?"

"Have we ever! Delilah and her friend decided it had to be cooler up in the mountains."

And safer, too, I thought. Another temporary dead end. There was no place to go but home. I dropped in at the station on the way back, but Bernie wasn't there; he was in court.

I had a new liar to add to the list—Joan Allingham. Unless her father had lied to her. Everybody was trying to break into my act.

"How about an omelet?" Mrs. Casey asked when I got home. "A nice ham-and-cheese omelet?"

"Splendid! Prefaced by a martini?"

"Each to his own," she said. "You make your martini. I'll stick with my regular."

The overcast drifted away; the sun came out. It was too hot to run and too soon after lunch to swim. It was dangerous to swim right after eating, my mother had often warned me. It led to cramps. That was probably a myth now, but there were very few things that my mother had told me that were not true.

She had died at the age of fifty-nine. The good die young.

I stretched out on a chaise longue in the shade. The weariness of frustration was bone-deep in me. But I wasn't about to quit. That, too, my mother had taught me.

I was dozing when the phone rang. It was Corey. "I've been talking with Mr. Detterwald. I think that you had better come up here tonight. Get here before dark."

"Why?"

"Something heavy is going down. The narcs are in town."

"I'll be there," I promised him.

Chapter Eighteen

WHEN Jan came home, I told her, "We're eating early tonight. Corey phoned from Donegal Bay. I'm going up there after dinner."

"It's about Mike Anthony, isn't it?" she asked.

"I guess."

"I talked with Daphne on the phone this morning," she explained, "and she told me Duane wasn't fit to live with. He's furious about the way Mike is acting."

"He has reason to be. His idiot friend has finally gone too far. I'll be seeing Duane, too."

"Good," she said. "You can bring back those samples that Daphne has decided are not for her."

My Jan, my practical Jan, a sensible woman in a crazy world.

The sky was unclouded, the sun still in command, when I drove up to Donegal Bay. In the east, the pale disc of a nearly full moon promised us light for tonight.

If something heavy going down was what I thought it was, Mike had picked the wrong night for it. He was leading with his overhand right again.

Both Detterwald cars and one other were on their driveway. I stopped there first.

Duane came to the door. "We're just having our coffee," he told me. "Join us." He led me to the living room at the rear of the house.

Daphne was sitting on a couch in front of a coffee table. Laura was looking out a full-length window that faced the sea. She didn't turn around when we came in.

"Coffee?" Daphne asked.

I nodded. "Black, please."

Laura turned, nodded at me, tried to smile—and left the room.

"God damn that Jeff!" Daphne said. "He doesn't deserve her."

Duane told me, "She said that Mike was using the boat tonight. I alerted the narcs."

"Is Jeff going with him?"

"We don't know," Duane said. "Laura hasn't seen him all day. Corey's out looking for him now. He's a sharp kid, that Corey, isn't he?"

"He is."

"A sharp kid," Daphne said contemptuously, "working for Alan Baker. A sharp, *crooked* kid."

"No!" I said.

She handed me my coffee. "Pardon me! But anybody who would work for Alan Baker is on my shit list."

"Calm down, Daphne," Duane said wearily.

"Look who's talking," she said. "Look who's talking calm down."

I sipped my coffee. Duane glared at his wife.

Daphne said, "I apologize, Brock. It's been a bad day. Duane and his stupid loyalties—first Mike and now Jeff."

"I can't think of Duane as stupid," I said, "and I've never considered loyalty a vice."

She smiled. "Damn you, you're so—so—"

"Loyal," Duane said. "Finish your coffee, Brock, and let's get the hell out of here. We'll take my car."

"While you're gone," Daphne said, "I'll put the samples I'm returning in Brock's. The day won't be a total loss."

"Women!" Duane said, as we walked to his car.

"Aren't they wonderful?" I said. "She's right, buddy. Sticking with Mike as long as you have is stupid."

"Don't I know it? But did you have to mention it?"

That was a pair of questions too complicated for me. They seemed to constitute a non sequitur. I didn't answer.

Corey was in his room when we got there. He told Duane, "I found Jeff. He and some fat guy with a crew cut are in that shack at the end of Surf Lane. Jeff brought some clothes with him."

"I know who he is," Duane said. "He's a friend of Jeff's. They played football together. Jeff isn't going out with Mike tonight. He's not *that* dumb. Did you spot the feds?"

"Some of them. Two of them are halfway up the bluff with binoculars. At least one of them is in those bushes near the pier. He was carrying a walkie-talkie."

"Have you seen Kronen?" I asked him.

"Not since noon. But I checked Anthony. He's still in the restaurant."

"Let's go to my office," Duane suggested. "We can see all the action from the porch. I brought my field glasses. This is the first time I've used them since I deserted the ponies."

The sun went down, the moon took over. There was no wind; the Pacific was pacific tonight, as smooth as a putting green. Overhead, the nine o'clock plane from San Francisco was heading for Los Angeles. To the south, the lights of a boat suddenly went dark.

"Probably the coast guard," Duane guessed.

A figure was walking along the beach now, heading for the pier. "It's Mike," Duane said. "He's alone."

There was the sound of an engine coughing into life, and then a boat came into view as it left the pier. Far out, on the course the boat was taking, a green light flashed on and off, and then a red light. And then we could see nothing but a shadow bobbing on the sea.

We waited. And waited. And waited some more.

"Damn it!" Duane said. "I wish I hadn't listened to my doctor. I need a cigarette. Don't either of you guys smoke?"

Corey and I shook our heads.

Then came the distant droning sound of a helicopter. It grew louder. A glaring spotlight suddenly came to life from the boat on the south, and flares went up and burst in the sky, flooding the area with brilliant light. From the sky, another searchlight was shining down from the helicopter.

"They got him," Duane said. "No boat is going to outrun that chopper. Let's go back to the house. One of the narcs promised that he would phone me."

"I'll stay here," Corey said. "I'm still working."

"I'm sure your client can read about it in the paper," I said.

"The paper isn't paying me," he said. "I'll stay here."

Duane was silent as we rode up the road to the bluff. He had to be hurting some inside. A long span of loyalty had been breached today.

His front door opened before we reached it. "What happened?" Laura asked.

"We're not sure yet," I told her. "But Jeff wasn't with him."

"They got Mike," Duane said. "I'm sure they got Mike. Let's have a cup of coffee and wait for the call."

Again we waited. And waited. Laura stood at the big window, looking down at the beach. Daphne read a book. Duane and I drank our coffee slowly, and waited.

Finally, I asked, "What's the phone number of that motel? I'll find out if Corey's there."

He looked up the number and gave it to me. Corey was there. "What happened?" I asked him. "That fed hasn't phoned."

"I can guess why," he said. "They blew it! They made their move too soon on the Mexican boat. *Before* the dope was transferred. They're holding Anthony for questioning. But where's their case? He had a right to be out on the ocean. He even had some fishing tackle with him."

"Are they still down there?"

"No. It's quiet now and I'm going to hit the sack. I'm bushed."

"Sleep well, Corey. You earned your rest."

"Well?" Duane asked.

I told him what had happened.

"That lucky puke!" Daphne said.

Laura said, "I hope it scares Jeff. I'd better go home now. He might be there."

Duane shook his head. "He's moved in with Butch Johnson."

"Sleep here tonight," Daphne urged her. "You can go down in the morning."

"Thank you, no," Laura said. "You never know with Jeff. I want to be there if he decides to come home." She left.

I asked Daphne, "Did you get the samples loaded?"

She nodded. "You didn't leave your car keys, so I couldn't open your deck. They're piled to the roof in the backseat. But I noticed you have outside rearview mirrors."

"I'll make it," I assured her, "unless somebody rear-ends me. Thanks for the coffee and the spirited dialogue. Why don't you two kiss and make up?"

"We will," she promised. "We always do."

Cyrus Reed Allingham would be as unhappy as Daphne was to learn that Mike had not been nailed on a narcotic smuggling charge. If Mike, as was probable, had paid for the dope in advance, he would be unhappier than both of them. Roughly half the money the kids had conned out of Felicia would be lost.

Unless, of course, Chico Maracho considered a prepaid-but-not-delivered purchase as a debt of honor. Considering his rap sheet, a debt of honor was probably a phrase that Chico didn't have in his vocabulary. And after the mauling Mike had given him in San Diego, Mike would not rank high on Chico's priority list of debtors.

Laura knew that Duane had tipped off the feds. If she told Jeff and he told Mike, there would be more fireworks in Donegal Bay. As Laura had said, you never knew with Jeff. He could now be closer with Mike than he was with her.

It was after midnight when I got home, but Jan was still up, watching a twenty-year-old western movie on the tube.

"What happened?" she asked. "Is Corey all right?"

"He's fine. He put in a long day at hard labor and is now

safely tucked away in his trundle bed. Your former school-mate almost got picked up by the narcotic boys, but he lucked out."

She stared at me. "You can't mean Duane. Was it Mike?"

"It was Mike. Duane tipped off the feds but, unfortunately, they moved too fast."

"Oh, God!" she said. "If Mike learns that Duane —" She didn't finish.

"My thought exactly. I brought the samples back. I'll unload them in the morning. Let's go to bed."

"You go," she said. "I want to see how this comes out."

"A crappy western? You are the sophisticated lady who sneers at me every time I watch them!"

"And you are the primitive gentleman," she countered, "who insists I must finish anything I start. I'll see you in the morning."

I took a warm shower and went to bed. The events of the evening tumbled around in my mind and lapsed into dreams I don't remember now.

I switched the samples from my car to Jan's in the morning before breakfast and picked up the morning paper from the lawn. The previous night's maritime adventure was not covered; they had gone to press before that.

I switched on the local radio station. The world news was being covered — riots, terrorist murders, revolutions, famines, and rest-home fires, all the cheerful morning fare that sets up a citizen for the dawning and demanding day.

The local news opened with the Donegal Bay story. Marijuana with a street value of three hundred thousand dollars had been seized. They love that phrase — "street value." It probably translated into the twenty-three thousand dollars left over after Jeff had bought the boat.

Mike Anthony, former middleweight contender and present Donegal Bay restaurateur, had been questioned by the officers but not held.

Jan went to work after breakfast. I had nowhere to go. I read the rest of the paper and went back to my notes. An image was beginning to take form in my mind — the image of the killer. But it was a doubtful image and would be difficult to prove.

There had been too many side roads in this quest, too many obscuring lies, misleading truths, and confusing alliances. The battle lines were clearer now. With Alan Baker, I was almost sure, it was jealousy that had prompted him to hire a detective. Max Kronen had undoubtedly switched employers for pecuniary reasons. And Felicia might have told me the truth; it could have been Allingham who had started the blackmail war. He was certainly the most vindictive.

I was still thinking of Felicia when the phone rang. It must have been an extrasensory moment. She said, "Alan and I would like to talk with you. Could we come over now?"

"I'll be home," I told her.

Chapter Nineteen

THEY were at the door twenty minutes later. Alan looked abashed, Felicia as spritely as ever. "Surprise!" she said. "We've come to join the good guys."

Several biting comments came to mind, but I said, "I'm glad. Was it a unanimous decision?"

"More mine than Alan's," she admitted. "Do we come in or stand out here like beggars?"

"I'm sorry. Come in."

We went into the living room. Alan took a chair in one corner of the room. Felicia sat on a couch next to me. "First of all," she said, "we want you to know that we had nothing to do with what almost happened to Mike last night."

"I believe that," I told her.

"And Alan lied to you," she went on. "When he first phoned you, he said he wasn't worried about whether I was back-dooring him with Mike Anthony. He was."

"I suspected that," I said. "And I believed you when you told me that Allingham started the blackmail war between you. Now, did you tell Alan about the money you gave Jeff and Laura to buy that charter boat?"

She nodded.

"Then tell me this — was it a loan or a payment for a piece of the action?"

Her face stiffened. "What are you suggesting, that I would get involved in narcotic traffic?"

"Only you know that. I asked the question because I can't believe you could even imagine that you might get your money back on what a charter boat could earn. Not if the money is split four ways."

She said coldly, "Our agreement reads that they will pay me twelve percent interest on the loan. If they never pay off the principal, that's all right with me. Neither Alan nor I have children."

"So you lent them fifty thousand dollars to buy a twenty-seven-thousand-dollar boat?"

She nodded. "The rest was for extending and repairing the pier."

"Laura told me the pier didn't need extending. Mike proved that last night. The boat was moored at the pier and left from there."

She stared at me and glanced at Alan. He said, "I told you they were conning you."

She sniffed. "What do you know about boats and piers?"

"Nothing," he admitted. "But I can spot con from a block away."

"And now," I said, "we come to the big question." I looked at Alan. "What is this blackmail ammunition you intend to use against Cyrus Allingham?"

His gaze met mine evenly. "I am not going to tell you that, because I no longer intend to use it. He made his move, sending Kronen down into Mexico to find that narcotic connection to Mike, hoping to involve Felicia. It backfired on him. I'm saving my ammunition for his next attack, if any."

"Does Lucy know what it is?"

He shrugged. "You'd have to ask her that. Did you find her?"

"No. She wasn't in Florian. I think she's on the run."

Felicia said, "Alan never asked for a dime from Mr. Allingham after he got the settlement money. Between us, Alan and I have more money than we are ever going to spend. If you want to confirm that, our accountant will give you all the information you need."

"I believe you," I said.

She smiled. "Would you still believe me if I couldn't prove it?"

"Don't flutter your eyelashes at him," Alan said wearily. "Any more questions, Brock?"

"One. How did you know that Max Kronen had gone to Mexico to investigate Mike's connection? He's working for Allingham."

"Farini told me. I never met this Kronen. But the picture I'm getting is that he may be working for Allingham but he is still reporting to Farini."

"That could be," I agreed. "Felicia, if you have any influence on Jeff, please use it. He has stopped listening to Duane."

"I will," she promised.

They hadn't told me much that was new, but they had confirmed what I suspected. It was logical that Max would turn double agent; it would double his income. That was *one* corner that I had never cut.

It was possible that the San Valdesto Police Department had put their investigation of the murder of Luther Barnum into the dead file. It was also possible they had learned some things that I had not. I went down there after lunch.

Bernie was standing at his front window, staring out at the traffic outside, an occupational habit of his when he wasn't hunched over his desk, elbow-deep in paperwork.

"Did you read about what happened in Donegal Bay last night?" he asked me.

"I saw it," I told him. "I was there."

He said, "It's tied up with Luther Barnum's murder, isn't it?"

"Peripherally. And maybe with your friend, Joe Farini. And with Cyrus Allingham and the Bakers. That's why Kronen was in Mexico, to find out about Mike Anthony's source. The source, I am almost sure, is a man named Chico Maracho."

"What a fount of information you are!" he said. "Sit down, and fill me in."

I sat down next to his desk and told him what I knew and guessed.

"Did you give all this to the sheriff's station up there?" he asked.

"No."

"Why not? You're still a citizen, aren't you?"

"You know I am. I thought you could tell them and earn yourself some county Brownie points."

"Sure you did!"

"Okay," I said, "I'll tell them. May I use your phone?"

"Never mind. I'll do it."

I smiled.

"Don't smirk at me, you smart-ass," he said. "We can't work the way you do."

"I know that. Now tell me what you know."

"Nothing. We're still looking for Barnum's killer."

"So am I. I located his cousin, the Allingham maid."

"Where? What's her address?"

I shook my head. "I'll handle it. To use your favorite line, it's outside your jurisdiction. And I don't want your ham-handed associates to blow it. Besides, at the moment she is not at that address."

He scowled at me.

"Trust me, Bernie," I said. "Have I ever given you reason not to?"

"Not often," he admitted. "To be frank about it, if we didn't think we could tie Barnum's murder to some chicanery of Farini's, we probably would no longer be investigating it."

"Ain't that the cynical truth? Some world, isn't it, buddy?"

"True. But it's the only one we have. Stay in touch, won't you?"

"I will. What would you do without me? I'll get you your captaincy yet."

"Your lack of modesty is nauseating," he said. "Get out of here!"

I went to Rubio's next, to learn if there was any new information my friends there had picked up. Court was not in session; The Judge was in bed with a summer cold, and it was Rubio's day off. His wife was behind the bar. I went home and phoned the Dunes Motel to learn if Corey was still up there.

He was, but not in his room now, the manager told me. He would be back at three o'clock. I gave the man my number and told him to have Corey phone me as soon as he came in. And added, "He can call collect."

The thought came to me after I had hung up—why was he still up there? Alan had admitted to Felicia that jealousy had been his reason for hiring Corey. The impression they had given me when they came to the house was that that was a thing of the past. Had he conned me again?

I had maligned the man. When Corey phoned (collect), he told me that Felicia was his new client. She had hired him to keep an eye on Jeff.

"Don't ask me why," he said. "He's got to be much too young for her, doesn't he?"

"That's not her reason. Has Jeff moved back with Laura?"

"Nope. She's running the store all by herself. Jeff went over to talk with Anthony for about an hour late this morning. Then he and that fat guy took off this afternoon along the beach in a dune buggy. I couldn't follow them through that sand, so I came back here."

"Have you seen Mr. Detterwald?"

"About twenty minutes ago. Man, is he steamed!"

"Go back there. Tell him to warn Laura that she shouldn't tell Jeff he had tipped off the narcs. It could get to Mike."

"Hell, *he* was going to tell Anthony. I think I talked him out of it. And I told Laura not to tell Jeff, if he ever comes back. She's some girl, isn't she?"

"Yes. Corey, you are more than a competent investigator. You are a citizen."

"I knew you'd approve," he said. "Besides, Mrs. Baker pays well."

He was developing into a well-balanced young man, with a genuine concern for people and a proper regard for the dollar. I had trained him well.

When Jan came home, she asked, "What's going on in Donegal Bay? I talked with Daphne just before I left the shop."

"And?"

"And she said Mike had been picked up for questioning again, and the sheriff's department up there was looking for Duane's nephew. His girl friend is being questioned by them now. Did you meet them when you were up there?"

Bernie had earned his Brownie points. I said, "I met them. She is a wonderful girl living with a stubborn jock."

"Just like us," Jan said. "And she mentioned that some man named Max Kronen is also being questioned. Isn't he a private investigator?"

"He is," I said. "They'll get blood out of a stone before they get any useful information out of Max Kronen. Do you have any samples you want me to take up there?"

She frowned. "Tonight? Are you going up there? Is Corey up there? Is that why you're going?"

"I'm going up there tonight," I said, "but not because of Corey. I'll probably stay overnight. I don't want to talk about it."

I phoned Corey and asked him if there were any vacant rooms at the motel. There were, he said; he could reserve me one. "But there's nothing going on right now," he said. "The feds are questioning Max Kronen, and the sheriff had released Anthony. I haven't been able to find Jeff."

"There's something going on. Get me a room."

Silence through our drinks, silence through dinner. Jan was miffed.

"Stop sulking," I said. "You were the one who encouraged me to go back to work."

"I know!" she said. "I've got the big-mouth disease. I must have caught it from you."

Some more silence, and then she said, "It's Corey, isn't it? That's why you are so concerned."

I shook my head. "It's Laura, Duane's adopted niece."

"And her boyfriend?"

"To hell with him," I said. "He doesn't deserve her."

Chapter Twenty

THE overcast was seeping in from the ocean, blanketing the stars, misting the moon. It would be a cold, damp night in Donegal Bay.

The feds had no case on Mike, the way I read it. If the sheriff had released him again, they must have realized the feds had no case. They had the Maracho connection now. Max would give them exactly as much information on that as would serve his present purpose. Putting Mike away would have earned him bonus money from Allingham, but Max hadn't come up with enough to take into court. If he had, Mike would now be in the slammer.

Maracho had not been on the boat when it was seized. The crew could make a deal with the feds for shorter time if they implicated the boss. If they didn't implicate the boss, they would get more expensive legal defense — and longer lives.

The Cad was in the Detterwald driveway, but not the Datsun. Daphne opened the door to my ring. "Thank God you're here," she said. "Did Jan tell you about what happened today?"

I nodded. "Isn't Duane home?"

"No. He's down at the office. At least he told me he was going there. Laura's here. She's resting. I gave her some sleeping pills. Damn that Jeff!"

"Is Laura being implicated?"

"No. She's in the clear. Aren't you coming in?"

I shook my head. I'm going down to talk with Duane."

"Please try to talk some sense into him!"

"I'll do my best," I promised.

There was patchy fog on the road down, short stretches of five-mile-an-hour clarity and then one-mile-an-hour blindness. The light was on in Duane's office.

He was sitting behind his desk. Corey was sitting in a rattan chair next to it, sipping a can of beer.

"Welcome to kook city," Duane said. "The town is crawling with crazies."

"Make sure you don't join them," I said. "Is Mike still in town?"

"I don't know. Your young friend here has convinced me not to make any foolish moves. But that dumb pug had better not come looking for me."

"Is that why you're down here at night, so he can find you? You want him to come looking for you, don't you?"

"Of course not! I came down here to get away from Daphne's tongue and have a couple of quiet drinks." He reached into a desk drawer and pulled out a bottle of bourbon. "Won't you join us?"

"Why not?" I said.

He poured me a stiff jolt in a tumbler, and one for himself. It didn't need ice or water; it was vintage sipping whiskey. I sipped.

Corey asked, "Why did Jeff run? They let Laura go."

"Laura didn't talk with Maracho," I pointed out. "Kronen probably told them that Jeff did."

There were footsteps on the porch and then the door opened.

"Speak of the devil," Corey said.

Max Kronen stood in the doorway. He glanced at me, at Corey, and then said to Duane, "I wanted you to know that I had nothing to do with involving your nephew or his nice girl friend in this mess, Anthony was the guy I was after."

Duane nodded.

"Pour him a slug of this good booze, Duane," I said. "The man is all worn out."

"I could use it," Max agreed. "Feds — Jesus, the arrogance of those bureaucrat bastards!"

Duane poured him a half tumbler of corn. Max sipped it.

"They really sweated you, huh?" I asked him.

"Did they ever! And then they released the report to the press that I had been *brought* in for questioning. I walked in! I volunteered. I gave 'em the Mexican connection."

"Did you see any money change hands down there or up here?"

"Not a dime. They don't have a case, but I gave 'em all I had. They'll probably blow a few more grand of taxpayers' money before they'll admit they don't have a case."

"I know what you mean," Duane agreed. "Almost every year the IRS sic their bloodhound accountants on me. They spend a couple thousand to squeeze another sixty or seventy dollars out of me."

Max sipped some more and licked his lips. "*This* is whiskey."

"Is Anthony in town?" I asked him.

"I don't know and I don't give a damn." He gulped the rest of his drink. "I'm going home." He grinned sourly at me. "You won't have Max to kick around anymore. But I guess I owe you, taking care of Anthony the way you did."

"Tell me, Max," I said, "do you really believe in that — owing and being owed?"

"I'd say yes," he said, "except that you wouldn't believe a goddamned thing I had to say, anyway. Thanks for the drink, Mr. Detterwald."

"Drive carefully," I said. "Go good home, Max."

"Screw you," he said, and walked out.

I was almost beginning to like the slob.

Corey said, "I'm going over to see if Jeff and Fatso have come back. I'll see you at the motel, Brock."

"I'll go with you," I said. "Duane, don't you think it's time for you to go home?"

He shook his head. "I'm overdue on my June quarterly tax estimate. I want to figure it close so those vultures can't sit on my money."

Outside, Corey said, "That was bull! He's waiting for Mike. I smell trouble."

"So do I. Let's hope it's Jeff he's waiting for. Why don't you check out Fatso's shack? I'll go over to the restaurant to see if Mike is back."

It was too misty to see into the Anchor from outside. I went in. A half dozen customers were drinking at the tables, but apparently no meals were being served. The door to the kitchen was open and it was dark in there. A waitress was behind the bar.

I asked her if she knew when Anthony would be back.

She shook her head. "Not before closing. He phoned and told me to close up. We close at midnight."

"Thank you," I said. "I'll see him in the morning. Does he live in that building behind the kitchen?"

"That's right. You're not a—a cop, are you?"

"No. An attorney. I'll see him in the morning."

Corey was waiting for me in the motel parking lot. "Jeff must be back," he said. "The dune buggy is parked in front of his place. Should we tell Mr. Detterwald?"

"No. He'd just rant and rave. I'll go over and talk with Jeff. You stay here."

It was the house closest to the beach on Surf Lane, he told me. "Now, watch that tongue of yours. They're a husky pair."

"I'll be careful, Papa," I promised.

The place was a sun-bleached structure of rough timbers and twelve-inch boards, set several feet above the ground on concrete blocks. A light glowed dimly through the two front windows.

There was no bell; I knocked.

Jeff opened the door. "Mr. Callahan! Did Uncle Duane send you?"

I shook my head. "Do you know the sheriff sent out a call to pick you up?"

"The sheriff? Why? Come in."

It was a one-room-and-bath house, smelling of fish. On a camper's gasoline stove set on a table in one corner, a bulky young man with a crew cut was stirring a pot of stew.

"This is Ted Johnson," Jeff said. "This is Brock Callahan, Butch."

I nodded a greeting.

"A pleasure," Butch said, and put a cover on the pot.

"The sheriff is cooperating with the feds," I explained to Jeff, "about that narcotic arrest last night. You weren't involved, I know, but it was your boat that was used. They questioned Mike again."

His friend said, "I think you'd better check in with the sheriff, Jeff. I'll go with you, if you want me to."

"I'd appreciate it," Jeff said. He looked at me. "We never left the beach. We were fishing up at the Puerta pier. Thank you for coming, Mr. Callahan."

"You're welcome. Jeff, make up with your uncle. Man, you are his pride and joy!"

He took a deep breath. "I will. Damn that Anthony! Laura was right about him. Do you know where she is? She isn't at the house."

"She's up with your Aunt Daphne, crying and waiting."

"I'll stop there and tell her I'm home," he said. "Let's go, Butch."

The dune buggy was already climbing the road to the bluff when I rejoined Corey.

I told him where Jeff was going and that he was going to stop in at the Detterwald house. "Tell Duane that. I'm going to my room and take off my shoes and watch TV. I've had too long a day for a forty-year-old man."

I was watching "Hill Street Blues" when Corey knocked on my door.

"I gave Mr. Detterwald your message," he told me, "but he's still in his office. I'm going to stay up for a while and keep an eye on him."

"You're not getting paid to watch him," I said. "Make out your report for Mrs. Baker and go to bed."

"Later," he said. "I like Mr. Detterwald. I don't want him to get into any trouble."

Corey might wind up with four employees someday. But he would never turn into a Max Kronen.

I tried to stay awake to see if there was any new development in the case on the eleven o'clock news, but my eyes refused to cooperate. Corey had the room next to mine. I didn't hear any sound from there before I fell asleep.

It was three minutes before two o'clock when I was awakened by a window-rattling crashing sound that seemed to come from the foot of the bluff. I got up and opened the door and looked out. All I could see was fog.

Corey's door opened and he came out to the runway. "What was it?" he asked.

"It sounded like a car went off that road to me. Maybe we'd better phone the highway patrol."

"I'll do it," he said. "Get your sleep, teach."

"What time did you get to bed?" I asked him.

"At one o'clock. Mr. Detterwald was still in his office, but I couldn't stick it out. It's too cold."

I went back to bed. At seven-thirty, he knocked on my door. "Hungry?" he asked. "I've got some instant coffee and doughnuts."

"Give me a couple of minutes. Did you phone the highway patrol?"

"I did. They said they'd check it. Let's eat in my room. It's nicer than this one. The furniture is newer."

"I'm not on an expense account," I explained.

We were on our second cup of coffee when we heard the sound of a siren coming from the direction of the bluff. We went out to the runway. We could see the red light flashing as the police car came down the winding road.

About a half a block from where we stood, a man and a woman in running clothes were looking down at the body of a man. He was lying on the sand across the street from Duane's office.

"Jesus!" Corey said. "Do you think —"

"Let's find out," I said.

It was Mike. He was wearing jeans and a sweat shirt. The sweat shirt was sodden with blood. His eyes were still open, staring blindly up at the murky sky.

Chapter Twenty-One

MIKE's body was gone, but two deputies and the local patrolman were still talking to the couple in running clothes when I went over to the tackle shop. Corey was in his room, phoning his report to Felicia.

Laura was alone in the shop. "Isn't it awful?" she said. "First Duane—and now this."

"Duane?" I asked. "What happened to him?"

"He went off the road last night. Didn't you hear the crash?"

I nodded. "Is he—is he...?"

"Lucky," she told me. "He must have been thrown clear before his car hit that big boulder at the bottom. The car was totaled. All Uncle Duane has are facial bruises and a broken nose."

I said nothing, thinking thoughts I didn't want to voice.

She asked, "Do you think Mike might have been killed by those Mexican friends of his? Maybe they think he double-crossed them. It was so vicious, using a knife!"

"He was stabbed to death?"

"Four times in the stomach, according to the patrolman who used our phone."

"It could be anybody," I said. "Do you have the key to Duane's office? I think I left my car keys in there last night. I can't find them anywhere else."

"I have a key." She reached under the counter, got a key, and handed it to me.

The letter opener wasn't on his desk or in any of the drawers, not in any place I searched in the office.

I took the key back to Laura and asked her, "Is Duane in the hospital?"

She shook her head. "He's home. Did you find your keys?"

"Yup. You know, you ought to take over the restaurant. Even Mike made a living there. And with the way you can cook—"

She frowned. "Mr. Callahan, that's macabre! I mean, it's so soon after...." She made a face.

"It's a macabre world, Laura," I told her, "and Mike is one man I can't mourn."

I went back to the motel. Corey was still talking with Felicia. When he had finished, I said, "Anthony was stabbed to death. And that letter opener of Duane's is missing. I checked."

His face stiffened. "That's none of our business."

"Of course it is! Don't make noises like Max Kronen. If you say nobody is paying us, I'll punch you in the mouth."

"Punch away," he said. "I am not going to be a party to putting Mr. Detterwald in jail."

"He'll have less chance of going there," I pointed out patiently, "if he turns himself in. That was his car we heard going off the road last night. The car was totaled. All Duane suffered was a broken nose and facial bruises. I'm going up to his house."

He looked up at the bluff. "You're probably guessing right. But I won't be a part of it. Mrs. Baker told me that I'm through here, now that Jeff and Laura are back together." He grimaced. "I'm sick! I should have stayed out there longer last night."

"No! You did more than duty called for. I'll see you back in town."

"Right," he said dully. "Luck."

He had started with a wife-tailing job and wound up in a murder case. His parents might reconsider their decision to let him go his own way. Not that it mattered; he was his own man now and would make his own decisions.

I checked out of the motel and drove up the winding road. The nagging thought came to me that Corey was right. It was none of my business. But I was no longer in business, and my intent was to advise Duane, not to expose him.

"Well," Daphne said, when she opened the door. "Another of the revelers! You don't look hung over."

I didn't ask what she meant. I, too, was a husband. "I've been drinking black coffee all morning," I explained. "How is Duane doing?"

"Better than he deserves. He's upstairs. It's the bedroom at the far end of the hall."

It was a large bedroom with double bathrooms. Duane looked doll-size in the enormous bed. His broken nose was taped, his left eye was swollen shut, his left cheek badly lacerated. In my Sherlockian view, he had been worked over by a mug or a pug with a heavy right hand.

"Are you going to make it, tiger?" I asked him.

"Hell, yes! I'm just resting. I'll be on my feet before tonight."

"Mike won't," I said.

His eyes glazed. "I heard about it. Somebody got to him with a knife. Maybe one of his narc friends?"

"Maybe. Were you drunk, or was it the fog?"

"Both," he said. His voice was guarded.

"Crashing into that rock at the foot of the cliff," I went on in my dumb but dogged way, "I can't understand how you walked away from that."

His voice was dead even. "I wasn't in the car when it hit the rock. I got thrown out halfway down."

I smiled at him.

"What is this?" he asked. "Are you playing cop for the insurance company—or what?"

"I'm playing friend, Duane. Did you lose your letter opener? I couldn't find it in your office."

"What the hell were you doing in my office?"

"Looking for the letter opener."

"That's how you play friend, accusing me of murder? Get out of here!"

I shook my head. "I came as a friend, and I came to talk sense. They'll find that letter opener. They'll match it up with the stab wounds. The reason you weren't in the car when it hit the rock is that you weren't in it when it went over the edge of the road. They'll put it all together, Duane."

"You're crazy!" he said. "You're absolutely bananas!" He pointed at his face. "You think Mike did this to me?"

"I do."

"Tell it to the cops," he said. "But get out of here. Friends like you I don't need."

"I'm not going to the cops, I said. "I'm not going to tell them you threatened me with that letter opener, or that you later told me you would stick it in Mike's throat. And you're not going to tell them that, either. You are going in with your attorney and tell them the way it happened. Unless you are as dumb as Mike was, and I don't think you are. Trust me, Duane."

"Trust you? Either I squeal on myself or you'll squeal on me. You call that trust? That's a threat."

"You weren't listening. I'm not going to turn you in. If you decide not to turn yourself in, I'm going home. You can lie here and wait for the sheriff."

He said nothing, looking at me thoughtfully.

I told him, "Corey stayed outside your office until one o'clock last night in that cold. He likes you. He was worried about you. He stayed out there freezing."

"He's a good kid," Duane said quietly.

"So am I. I'm on your side."

Silence for seconds. And then he said, "That bastard! He came to the door just before I was ready to go home. He said, 'Come out here, Weasel, and get what's coming to you. You blew the whistle on me, you slimy midget. Come out here where the sand will soak up your blood.'"

"That would have been a smart time to pick up the phone on your desk and dial nine-one-one," I said.

"I was mad and drunk. I was not thinking smart."

"Did he hit you first?"

He pointed at his nose. "Right here. And I stuck the opener into his belly and he got a couple more shots in while I stuck him again. And then he went down."

"And then," I finished for him, "you got in your car, still drunk and dazed, and headed for home in the fog—and went over the edge."

"You mean I should lie about that part?"

I nodded. "We may be citizens, Duane, but we're not saints. You didn't even remember most of it until right now, when you phoned your attorney."

"Okay," he said. He reached over to the bedside table and picked up the phone.

I went downstairs. Daphne was waiting there. She asked, "Did he admit it?"

"He did. He's phoning his attorney. Did you know?"

"Not last night," she told me. "Not until ten minutes ago, when I took the garbage out—and saw the letter opener in the garbage can. Has he got a case, Brock?"

"I think so. Self-defense. Mike attacked him with two lethal weapons, according to California law—his fists."

"Will you stay around for a while?"

"Of course," I said.

His attorney came with a plainclothes officer about forty-five minutes later. The officer was probably a deputy. They went upstairs. Daphne and I sat in the living room, drinking coffee and thinking our separate thoughts.

About half an hour later, they came down the stairs again. The detective left; the attorney came into the living room. He was classy, a tall, English-type guy, wearing a virgin-wool suit in some rough textured weave. I've forgotten his name.

"It looks promising," he told Daphne. "The federal narcotics officers are willing to testify that Duane was working with them. And the sheriff told me, off the record, that this Anthony person has had several assault charges filed against him."

When he left, Daphne said, "Promising, but not certain."

"To doctors and lawyers," I explained, "promising means certain. But if they said certain, they couldn't charge as much."

"I hope you're right." She stared at the floor. "It's a terrible thing to say, but I can't feel sad because Mike's dead."

"It's a feeling we share," I said. "Go up and solace your husband. I'm going home."

She kissed me on the cheek. "Thanks for everything, Brock."

Corey's job was finished, and Kronen had gone home. My quest had been interrupted; it might never be successful. Mr. Ultimate Morality of Veronica Village had been stymied by Mike's death; his war with Alan Baker was temporarily at a halt. And Alan would no longer have cause to worry about Mike and Felicia. He had benefited the most from the whole sordid affair, almost as if he had engineered it.

What in hell was any of it to me? Baker had come out on top and Duane might be headed for the slammer. Fine work, peeper!

It was noon, but I wasn't hungry. This might be one of the days when Bernie ate lunch in his office. I drove to the station.

He was there, eating a sandwich. "Pastrami and cheddar cheese," he told me. "Want one?"

"No, thanks. I came for soul food."

"You'll have to go further down Main Street to find that. What's bugging you now?"

I sat in the chair next to his desk. "Mike Anthony was killed last night."

"I know. So?"

"I knew who did it. I convinced him to confess, which he did. It was self-defense, so he might get off, but what if he doesn't? A creep is killed, and a citizen might go to the can for it."

"And you feel guilty about that? It is illegal for goys to feel guilty. That's restricted to my tribe." He smiled at me. "Brock, don't think too much. It discombobulates you. Instinct, that's your strength. Go with your strength!"

"I guess you're right. I have a feeling I know who killed Luther Barnum, but I can't prove it. When the showdown comes, I might need you to go along."

He smiled again. "I'll be ready. That's what friends are for."

"Thanks for the soul food," I said.

Chapter Twenty-two

BERNIE was an ally. Bernie was a comfort. Though we squabbled with each other like victims of an unfortunate marriage, when push came to shove, as it had in the past, Bernie was there to support me.

He didn't often approve of my investigative techniques, and I often grew impatient with his rigid bureaucratic code. I had to remind myself that he was *the law;* his code of conduct was determined by that.

And I had to admit that he was more perceptive than I, more careful to avoid rash judgments and emotional decisions. As I have said too often before, we yo-yos have to follow our instincts.

From his office, I drove down to Rubio's. The Judge was back on his bench.

"Are you feeling better?" I asked him.

"Much better, thank you. Are you buying?"

"Be my guest."

"A bottle of Beck's," he said to Rubio.

Rubio looked at me. "A double bourbon," I said, "with a dash of water. And whatever you want, on me."

He served us and poured himself a cup of coffee. He asked, "Have you learned anything new on what happened to Luther?"

"Nothing certain. But I have a hunch. That's mostly what I work on. You must have noticed that I am not an intellectual."

Rubio shook his head. "I never noticed that."

The Judge said, "You graduated from Stanford. That is quite possibly the finest university west of Massachusetts. What you mean is that you are not one of those pretentious men who has been educated beyond the limit of his intelligence."

"This hunch you got," Rubio asked. "Do you want to name a name?

"Not yet. I could be wrong."

The Judge said, "I would be willing to wager eight to your three that you are right. Is it connected with what happened in Donegal Bay last night?"

"Peripherally," I said.

Rubio frowned. "What does 'peripherally' mean?"

"It means 'kind of' to you," The Judge informed him. "In this instance it means 'away from the center.' Brock, you stick with this. The police don't give a damn about anything that happens to any of us down here. Unless they think they can jail some black for it."

"It wasn't a black," I said.

"Then you're going it alone. You're all we have. Stay with it."

I stopped at the Bakers' on the way home. Alan knew more than he had told me at the house; he had admitted it. I hoped to convince him to share his ammunition with me.

The Bakers, the maid informed me at the door, had gone up to San Francisco late that morning for rest and relaxation. The man who had been killed the night before, she explained to me, had been Mrs. Baker's dearest friend.

"She must have got the name wrong," I said. "It was Mike Anthony who was killed."

"That's the man. I don't understand what you mean, sir."

"Work on it," I told her. "I'll bet she'll miss his funeral."

She was still standing in the open doorway when I got into my car. What an ass I was, taking out my frustration on a non-combatant.

Mrs. Casey was in her room when I came home, watching her second favorite soap opera. Even kooky Karl Marx had not anticipated that his opiates for the masses would ever sink to that level.

I went out in back and tried to nap. But the blind eyes of

Mike Anthony intruded on my reverie, and the soiled blue flannel robe of Luther Barnum.

There were a number of fingers pointing in the same direction: the cognac, the guarded back door at the Travis Hotel, the scandal-sheet reporter, the nonprofessional print on the bottle, and the lies I had uncovered.

They all pointed at my choice for the killer. But juries demand more than clues, except in TV mysteries. Real-life juries demand solid evidence.

I was dozing when the phone rang. It was Joe Farini. "I realize," he said, "knowing your opinion of me, that I might be making a futile phone call. But Alan Baker told me you were trying to find Lucy Barnum and I wondered if you'd had any success."

"Any enemy of Cyrus Allingham can't be all bad," I assured him. "I haven't had much success so far, but a former associate of mine in Santa Monica has located a close friend of hers down there. He's checking it out now."

"If you learn anything, Brock, I would appreciate a call."

"You'll get it. I want to help Alan build up his stockpile of ammunition so that we can destroy that bigoted bastard."

"Don't we all?" he said. "Thanks, Brock."

Alan was worried that I might find Lucy and take the powder out of his ammo. Secrecy was all he had to sell. Either he or Farini had probably phoned Delilah Kent in Florian and discovered she wasn't there. I had told Alan that Lucy wasn't there. If I could reveal his secret, he would have nothing to bargain with. He wouldn't be the only winner in this war.

When Jan came home, I told her the story of my night in Donegal Bay.

"If Duane's in trouble," she said, "I had better phone Daphne. I was supposed to go up there tomorrow, but it might be an intrusion, under the circumstances."

When she came back from her phone call, she told me, "Duane isn't being held. He was released on his own recognizance, whatever that means."

"It means that Duane is saving bail money. It probably means that the DA up there has realized he doesn't have a strong case. And I'm sure that Mike Anthony was not one of the area's most admired citizens."

"Mike is dead," she said, "and Duane won't be tried. Corey's job is finished. Mr. Kronen has gone home. And what about you?"

"I haven't quit. I want to know who killed Luther. The police will drop the investigation the minute they learn they can't tie the murder to Farini."

"Are you saying that the police don't care but you do?"

I nodded. "Shouldn't I care?"

"I don't know if you should or you shouldn't," she answered. "But I am glad that you do."

It would be easy to rationalize my quest for the killer as concern for the underprivileged. That could make a man feel noble. But the truth was that if Luther had been as rich and vindictive as Cyrus Allingham, I would stay on the hunt. My motive was primitive; *nobody* should get away with murder.

Driving to Florian on Friday morning, I dreamed up and discarded a number of approaches that might influence Lucy Barnum to confide in me. The truth seemed to be the best approach; I was investigating the death of her cousin. If she wanted to know why, a half truth would serve; I was working with the San Valdesto Police Department.

It was ten-thirty when I rang the doorbell at the home of Delilah Kent. There was no response. I went next-door to see if her neighbor was home. She came to the door in a different pair of tight shorts, but the same bulging halter.

She smiled at me. "I remember you. The book salesman."

I smiled back at her. "I lied to you, ma'am. I'm working with the San Valdesto Police Department on the murder of Luther Barnum. It was Miss Kent's houseguest I came to see. I don't normally lie, but I thought the truth might be dangerous for Lucy Barnum. And also, possibly, Miss Kent."

She studied me for a moment. Then, "Come in. It's too hot to stand out there. I've just made a pitcher of lemonade. Would you like some?"

"I'd love some. If you want to check my credentials, you could phone Lieutenant Bernard Vogel at —"

"No need," she interrupted. "I can tell an honest face when I see one."

The living room she led me into was smaller and less southern than Marilyn's up in Donegal Bay. But the motif was similar — hooked rugs and maple furniture with Norman Rockwell prints on the walls. "New England provincial" would best describe it.

I was sitting in a maple chair when she brought me a tall glass of lemonade from the kitchen. She handed it to me and sat with her own glass in a matching chair.

"Luther grew up here, too," she told me, "though, of course, he was a lot older than Lucy. He had a hardware store in town. But then his wife died and he took to drink. He lost everything, the house and the store. They didn't have any kids of their own. Lucy was very close to him, more like a daughter."

"That's the picture I got," I said. "She sent him money, and paid for his membership in a funeral society. I suppose you know that Lucy works for Cyrus Allingham."

She nodded. "Is he involved in Luther's murder?"

"He could be. He's a strange man. Luther might have known something about him that..." I paused.

"That Luther could blackmail him about?" she asked.

"Possibly."

"Not the Luther I knew," she said. "But once a man has taken to drink, who knows? Do you think Mr. Allingham fired Lucy because of that? Is that why she's here with Delilah?"

"I didn't know she was fired. The story I got in Veronica Village from Joan Allingham is that her father sent Lucy to Hawaii for a vacation. That turned out not to be true."

She said acidly, "Her father probably lied to her. The lies that man prints in his sickening publications! They're worse than those scandal magazines they sell in supermarkets."

I told her, "There was a reporter from one of those magazines who came to see Luther a short time before he died."

"Maybe Mr. Allingham sent him."

"No. I think he wanted to learn what Luther knew. Evidently, he never learned it. Was Delilah Lucy's best friend in high school?"

"Maybe her only friend. Lucy was not an outgoing girl in high school, and neither was Delilah. Then Delilah went on to college, and Lucy's family couldn't afford to send her. She went into domestic work."

"I wonder when they'll be home," I said.

"It should be soon. I got a card from Delilah. They planned to be home before noon. You can wait here, if you want. It's too hot outside. Another glass of lemonade?"

I had that while I waited, plus the story of her life. She had buried a husband in Vermont and had come to California for a change of scene — and possibly luck. But she had put on weight in this lush land, so it now seemed that a second marital alliance was unlikely.

"I always liked a man around the house," she said, "but to tell you the truth, they can be a nuisance, too. I'm beginning to enjoy my freedom."

"That's my wife's view of it," I said. "That's why we both decided to go back to work. Couldn't you find a part-time job in town, just for the variety?"

"I have one," she told me. "I help Delilah out at the library." She looked past me, out the window. "Oh, there they are now. Good luck, Mr. Callahan."

I thanked her for the lemonade and her hospitality and went out to my car. I sat in there until they had unloaded their sleeping bags and camping paraphernalia from the Chevette hatchback before I went up to ring the doorbell.

The name Delilah Kent had engendered in me a vision of one of those languid, tawny British lovelies you see in their films. But this Delilah was not one of those. Her coal-black hair hung down in two long, tight braids. Her face was faintly

Oriental, suggesting some American Indian ancestors. She was slim and tall, and she stood as erect as a Marine drill sergeant.

"Miss Kent?" I asked.

She nodded.

"My name is Brock Callahan," I said. "I'm working with the San Valdesto Police Department on the murder of Lucy Barnum's cousin. I came here to talk with her."

There was the sound of hurried movement in the house behind her and then the slam of a door.

"I doubt if Lucy will talk with you," she said. "She wouldn't talk about it with me, and we've been friends for a long time."

"Is she still working for the Allinghams?"

"No. She quit. She was secretive about her reasons for that, too."

"She's going to have to talk with the police eventually," I pointed out. "I am not a police officer—more of a consultant to them. If you would phone Lieutenant Vogel in San Valdesto, he will confirm that."

"I'm sure that won't be necessary," she said. "Come in, Mr. Callahan."

Chapter Twenty-three

SPARTAN would be the word for the Kent cottage. We walked through a sparsely but adequately furnished living room to a combination small breakfast room and large kitchen.

"Have you had lunch?" she asked me.

"No. But don't bother."

"It's no bother. I have to keep busy! I'm worried about Lucy. I never could understand why she would work for a malignant cretin like Cyrus Reed Allingham. And I never thought the day would come when she wouldn't confide in me."

I sat on a bench in the breakfast nook. "I think she's scared and running," I said. "I didn't come here to harass her. I'm a retired private investigator and not being paid. Trying to learn who killed her uncle is mostly an avocation with me."

"Why?" she asked.

"I don't know," I admitted. "Maybe it's vindictive. I hate killers."

"That's one of the better hates," she said. "All we seem to have in the house are eggs and leftover ham and rolls. How about a ham omelet?"

"Perfect," I said.

"But first," she decided, "I am going to get Lucy out here. Luther was our best friend in this town. This is nonsense!" She left the kitchen.

I heard her say, "Lucy, unlock this door right now! Our visitor is not working for Mr. Allingham. He's looking for Luther's killer. Isn't that important to you?"

Half a minute later, they both came into the kitchen. This

was the woman Baker had tried to make time with, and the kind he could con. She was fairly short and her figure was all woman. Her big, trusting brown eyes were wet with tears.

She said defiantly, "I don't know who killed Luther. All I know is that a man named Joseph Farini was trying to blackmail Mr. Allingham. Why can't you leave me alone?"

"His murder could be connected with the blackmail," I said. "I'm not investigating that — only the murder. The police have given up on it. Please believe that I'm not here to harass you."

She slid onto the bench across from me. "Some of the men Mr. Allingham had working for him —" She took a breath. "Any one of them could have done it."

"Yes. Alan Baker told me the same thing. But they have been questioned, I'm sure, by the police. At least I know that a thug hired by Farini has."

"How about Alan Baker? Did they question him?"

"I don't know. I have reason to dislike Alan Baker, but I can't see him as a killer. Mr. Allingham would be a more likely choice. But don't you see — first we have to have a reason, we have to learn what the blackmail was about."

"Alan Baker would be the man to ask that."

"I did. He refused to tell me. He said that now that Mr. Allingham's counterthreat had failed, he was no longer interested in him. Mr. Allingham admitted to me that he was going to fight fire with fire, as he put it. That means he had learned something about Mr. Baker, too."

She said, "He would. I don't know how Joan can bear to live with that man. Did you see her when your were up there? How is she?"

From the corner of my eye, I saw Delilah turn quickly from the sink to look our way. What I saw in her eyes confirmed the hunch that had started me along this final line of inquiry.

"They're not at all alike, Joan and her father," Lucy said. "Joan is thoughtful and charitable and —"

"Lucy, for heaven's sake!" Delilah said.

Lucy glared at her, and tears welled again in her eyes.

"I'm sorry," Delilah said softly. "I'm as overwrought as you are. It's going to be all right, Lucy. You're home now, where you belong. Please don't cry."

She started to make the omelet. Lucy stared at the top of the table. I was silent; enough had been said. The picture was complete. I knew, now. But what did I have that would stand up in court?

The omelet was tasty, the rolls crisp, the talk over the table was general. So long as I was sitting with a librarian, I mentioned the trouble I was having trying to understand William Faulkner.

Delilah tried to explain that complicated genius to me, and failed, as the other literate friends of mine had. We went from there to the weather, and then I bid them good-bye and headed for the station and my soul-food brother.

I laid it all out for Bernie, all the bits and pieces that pointed a finger.

"An interesting pattern of Gaelic hunches and Celtic intuitions," he admitted. "But what if the judge isn't Irish?"

"Don't give me that schtick! It's a case!"

"Completely circumstantial," he pointed out. "Do you have any solid evidence?"

I looked at him coolly. "You forgot the unidentified fingerprint, Hawkshaw."

"By God, I did!" he said. "Hell, yes, we've got that for the clincher." He chewed his lip and frowned. "But do we have enough here to give us reasonable cause to bring a suspect in?"

"I don't know. That's your department."

"The sheriff up there," he explained, "has never been cooperative with us, particularly when it involves one of his socialite citizens. I don't have any clout with him at all."

"How about Chief Harris?" I suggested. "He's a socialite type."

Bernie nodded. "He's our best bet, if he'll go along with it. He's at a Rotary luncheon now. I'll ask him when he gets back and phone you. Will you be home?"

"I'll be home. I'll dream up some excuse for our visit while I'm waiting. You could call up there to see if Allingham will be home. Do you have his unlisted number?"

Bernie nodded. "He gave it to one of the officers who went up to question him. But what's my excuse for calling him?"

"Tell him you have some information on the death of Luther Barnum that you hope he can verify. Tell him you have been maintaining a surveillance on Joe Farini and hint that he's your prime suspect."

He frowned. "Why that bit?"

"So we can get in. It will put the old sourpuss off guard."

He sighed. "Gad, the way you work!"

"There's a word for the way I work," I told him.

"Deviously?"

"No. Successfully."

"Go!" he said. "Take your arrogance with you."

I went. It had been a nasty case full of tawdry people. I wasn't looking foward to that night. But the background on Luther Barnum that I had picked up in Florian bolstered my conviction that his murderer shouldn't get away with it.

Bernie phoned around four o'clock. "Chief Harris," he told me, "is not friendly with the sheriff up there. But he is with the watch commander who will be in charge tonight. Harris phoned him at home. The commander will send a deputy along with us."

Jan came home from Donegal Bay with the best news of the day. The district attorney had finally decided he didn't have a strong case; Duane would not be prosecuted.

I told her where I was going and why.

"Is this the third act?" she asked. "Does the curtain come down tonight?"

"Maybe."

"I'd like to wish you luck," she said, "but it only means that tomorrow you'll be restless again, fretting for something that will keep you occupied."

"Not anymore," I told her. "I can always deliver samples."

Bernie picked me up at seven o'clock. "This could be a wild

goose chase," he complained, "and I'm not even going to get regular or overtime pay for it."

"How come?"

"I explained your theory to the chief and he was doubtful about it. So I am not *officially* on the trip. But, he assured me, if I wanted to accompany my good friend, he would understand."

"What a compassionate man he is! If we luck it out, we can issue a joint press release. It could go: 'Despite the protestations of Chief Chandler Harris of the San Valdesto Police Department, Lieutenant Bernard Vogel and his astute associate—'"

"Oh, shut up!" he said.

Chapter Twenty-four

THE sheriff's station was located about midway between Donegal Bay and Veronica Village. We picked up the plainclothes deputy there. His name was Harold Pointer. He was a middle-aged, middle-sized man with prematurely gray hair.

"Haven't I seen you somewhere?" he asked as he climbed into the car.

"At the Detterwald house," I said. "I was there when you and Duane's attorney came to the house."

"That's it," he agreed. "Were you involved in that, too?"

"There could be a connection," I said. "I understand Duane isn't going to be prosecuted."

"He isn't, and I'm glad. Anthony has been nothing but trouble since he moved in. We don't need his kind up here."

I didn't ask him if they needed the Cyrus Allingham kind. The area was probably loaded with the breed.

"Ye gods!" Bernie said when the castle came into view. "Is that for real?"

"It's our San Simeon," Pointer said. He stepped out of the car. "I'll phone." He went to the phone booth.

"We can get in," Bernie said, "but can we get out?"

"If you and Pointer are armed, we might escape. But watch out for the moat. Allingham told me it's mined."

"Is the man crazy?"

"Only to us," I said. "We're the immoral minority."

Down went the drawbridge, up went the portcullis. The door was open when we walked toward the house. The tall figure of

Cyrus Allingham was outlined by the light from the entry hall behind him.

"Good evening, Harold," he said to Pointer. And then he saw me. "What are you doing here? I've heard some disturbing things about you since last we talked, Mr. Callahan."

I didn't answer.

Pointer said, "We're not here to harass you, Mr. Allingham. This is Lieutenant Vogel of the San Valdesto Police Department. He assured me that we are here only for any helpful information you might have about the death of Luther Barnum."

Allingham said stiffly, "I have no information that could help. Our maid might have, but she's in Hawaii."

"No, she isn't," I said. "I talked with her this morning."

He glared at me, scowled at Pointer, and said, "Come in."

Joan was sitting at the far end of the living room. She didn't get up as we entered. "Good evening, Harold," she said.

I was getting the uneasy feeling that Harold wasn't on our side. I said, "Good evening, Joan."

She ignored me. She asked Harold, "What is he doing here?"

Bernie said, "You could call it a citizen's complaint. If we are intruding, we will leave. But I think you would be better served if we stayed. Mr. Callahan is not a scandalmonger."

"Scandal?" Allingham asked. "Did I hear you correctly, sir?"

"You did," Bernie said evenly. "One of those scandal-sheet reporters interviewed Lucy Barnum's cousin at his hotel."

Joan glanced worriedly at her father, and then at me.

"Luther told him nothing," I said. "Luther's secret died with him."

Allingham looked at Pointer. Pointer shrugged. Allingham said, "I don't like this."

"Perhaps," Pointer said, "it would be wise to have your attorney here."

Allingham shook his head. "Let's sit down."

We sat at the other end of the room from Joan. Allingham looked coldly at me. "Speak your piece, Mr. Callahan."

"Luther," I opened, "was probably killed by a person who

was familiar with the rear-door entrance to the second floor of his hotel. The prostitutes who live on that floor do their soliciting near that doorway. Only their customers can get to the second floor by that staircase. Luther probably told Lucy about it."

"Did she tell you that," Allingham asked, "when you talked with her this morning?"

"No. Because I didn't ask her. I didn't pry. She was so troubled, so close to panic, I thought it would be cruel. And I doubt if she would have told me if I had asked."

"Good!" he said.

"About the customer who came to that door the night Luther was killed, the girl told me she thought he was a mute. He didn't talk. He paid her and went to her room. Then, while she was getting undressed, he suddenly walked out."

"I'm not following you," Pointer said. "Is that the man you think Mr. Allingham might know about?"

"It might not be a man," I said. "That's why he didn't talk. A woman posing as a man wouldn't risk talking."

Pointer's smile was cynical. "You're really far out, aren't you? Is that all you have, these kookie theories?"

"Let's hear the rest," Allingham said.

"The customer," I went on, "had a bulge under the field jacket he, or she, was wearing. It might have been a bottle of cognac. The killer might have taken that poisoned liquor down to Luther's room on the same floor. He, or she, might have been somebody Luther knew, or knew of. Most tenants in that hotel don't open their doors to strangers that late at night."

"Might, might, might," Pointer said scornfully. "All maybes, no meat, no case."

"Why don't you shut up?" Bernie said. "Why don't you keep your brown nose out of this?"

"Don't tell me to shut up," Pointer said. "I'll—"

"Be quiet, Harold," Allingham said. "Go on, Mr. Callahan."

"When I talked with Joan," I said, "she kept insisting that the information Alan Baker was threatening you with was probably some financial manipulation she didn't understand. She was trying to throw me off the trail. What Baker knew had nothing to do with finance. And she told me Lucy was in Hawaii. That, we now know, was a lie."

"I lied about it, too," Allingham admitted. "But certainly not to cover up a murder. My God, are you accusing Joan of that, of murder? I don't know what you have learned about her or her relationship with Lucy, but accusing her of murder is absurd!"

"Not if she was trying to protect you," I pointed out. "She knew what a scandal-sheet story would do to you and your cause." I looked at Joan. "Luther would never have given the reporter the story he was hoping for. He loved Lucy."

A silence.

Then Pointer asked, "What's going on here? What's this about relationship?"

Nobody answered him.

I said, "When I talked with Luther, he said he knew why Lucy had stayed with Joan after the divorce, but that was another story. It was a story he would never tell anybody. He knew she was a lesbian when she was still living in Florian. But I repeat—he loved her."

From the other end of the room, Joan said, "The night Luther was killed, I was asleep right here. My father will attest to that."

"Not under oath," he said wearily. "You were down at that benefit concert in San Valdesto. At least that's what you told me. It is time to stop lying, Joan."

He looked at me. "We have lied, both of us, but we're not murderers. You have come up with a damaging set of suppositions, I'll admit. But you have no real evidence, have you?"

"That's for sure," Pointer said.

"We have a fingerprint," Vogel said. "We lifted it off that cognac bottle. I brought the print with me. If it doesn't match Miss Allingham's, you are right. We don't have a case."

Allingham looked at his daughter and back at Vogel. "We'll

go to the sheriff's station tomorrow for the fingerprint check. The rest, the other thing that has been mentioned here tonight, there is no need to reveal that, is there?"

Vogel shook his head. "Your daughter's sexual preferences are no concern of mine. But murder is. I think we should check the fingerprint tonight."

"No need for that," Pointer said. "Tomorrow will do as well. The understanding we got from your chief was that you were coming up here for information, not to make an arrest."

Vogel glared at him.

"Call the station if you want," Pointer said. "Captain Walsh is in charge. You know him, don't you, Lieutenant?"

"I know him," Vogel admitted. "He could be your twin." He turned to Allingham. "What brand of cognac do you serve your guests, sir?"

"Spanerti."

"That was what we found in Barnum's room. And there isn't a liquor store in San Valdesto that sells it. Do you buy it locally?"

Allingham shook his head. "It is not available locally. I buy it from the importer in San Francisco."

"And strychnine?" Vogel asked. "Is that available locally?"

Allingham's face stiffened at the scorn in Vogel's voice. He said, "Our gardener uses it. He mixes it with chopped meat for the rats that have been troubling us."

"I'll want to see him tomorrow," Vogel said. "Make sure that he is available."

Allingham said, "We'll all be here, Lieutenant. You have my word on that."

We left. As we got into the car, Pointer said, "I suppose you think I am a goddamned toady."

Vogel didn't answer. He started the engine.

Silence. We drove out over the drawbridge. We drove about a hundred feet down the long driveway before Vogel pulled over onto the grass and turned out the lights.

"Now what?" Pointer asked.

"Tomorrow!" Vogel said acidly. "She could be in Argentina by tomorrow."

"You don't know the old man like I do," Pointer argued. "He's no liar. He didn't have to tell you about the strychnine, but he did. And the cognac, too."

"I'm not after him," Vogel said. "I'm waiting for her."

"So we sit," Pointer said. "Did either of you guys bring a bottle?"

We didn't answer.

"I'll tell you how sure I am," Pointer said. "If she comes down this driveway tonight, I'll make the collar myself."

Forty-five minutes later, a Mercedes with the lights off rumbled over the drawbridge and started down toward us.

Vogel switched on the car lights and pulled over to the center of the driveway. "Here she comes," he said. "It's your collar, Pointer.

On the drive home, Vogel said, "They sure take care of their own up here, don't they?"

"Yup. We would have looked like a pair of damned fools if that print hadn't matched, wouldn't we?"

"I wouldn't. I only came along for the ride."

"And the credit," I said. "Not that it will make you very popular in Veronica Village. But you still rank high with the boys here for the Donegal Bay information you fed them. I suppose Joan Allingham will be tried in San Valdesto."

He nodded. "They're on the way to pick her up right now. And who do you think is going to defend her? Farini!"

"It's a crazy world," I said.

"They're all nuts," he agreed. "Everybody but us."